TEXAS FIRE

He was waiting for her in the room. He kicked the door shut as he grabbed her. Pratt chuckled. "You can fight it, or you can just settle back and enjoy it. Don't matter. You're going to get it, either way."

Suddenly the door seemed to disintegrate in an explosion of splintered wood. Pratt whirled and triggered one barrel of the scattergun. It missed and Shell was on him, knocking the shotgun to the floor. Whipping his longcoat aside, Pratt drew his six-shooter. Up on one knee, Shell was drawing the Remington. They fired almost simultaneously. Shell didn't even feel the bullet graze his rib cage. Pratt doubled over, clutching at his belly. Emmy retrieved the shotgun and raised it to chest level and fired. The impact punched Pratt through the window. His corpse hit the boardwalk roof and fell through to land on the weathered planks below.

By Hank Edwards

Published by HarperPaperbacks

RIDE FOR RIMFIRE

HANK EDWARDS

HarperPaperbacks
A Division of HarperCollinsPublishers

This is a work of fiction. The characters, incidents, and dialogues are products of the author's imagination and are not to be construed as real. Any resemblance to actual events or persons, living or dead, is entirely coincidental.

HarperPaperbacks   *A Division of* HarperCollins*Publishers*
10 East 53rd Street, New York, N.Y. 10022

Cover illustration by Tony Gabriele

First printing: February 1995

Printed in the United States of America

HarperPaperbacks and colophon are trademarks of HarperCollins*Publishers*

❖ 10 9 8 7 6 5 4 3 2 1

1

The day was dark and dismal. Thunder rolled across the Texas hill country. Lightning flickered out of the black bellies of low-hanging clouds scudding south toward Mexico. The rain was a constant misery, sometimes a drizzle, sometimes whipping up into a furious downpour drenching the *brasada* in driving silver-gray sheets.

On the rock-strewn slope of a ridge near the San Saba Road, a congregation stood in the nightlike gloom, gathered beneath a stand of several stately oaks. In the distance, across the serpentine river, pin-pricks of buttery light marked the town of Lampasas, three miles distant. Beneath the trees stood two head-stones.

These quiet mourners stood about an open grave, clustered beneath a canvas tarpaulin lashed to poles that quivered in the gusting wind. The tarpaulin did little to keep them dry, or the grave from filling with water. Rivulets cascaded down the red flanks of the six-foot hole. Forty people were in attendance, a dozen of them Rimfire cowboys. The others had come from town to pay their last respects.

The casket lay beside the grave. A couple of mud-smeared cowboys stood near it, leaning wearily on pick and shovel, mounds of dirt at their feet. The preacher stood beside the headstone, which was already in place. On the stone was etched:

SAMUEL GUNNISON
1809–1875
TEXAN CLEAR THROUGH

The others, their dark suits and dresses protected by rain-glistening slickers of yellow, black, and white, stood solemnly listening as the preacher concluded his service. Having quoted from Psalms without benefit of Bible, the Reverend Gillum peered at the faces of the people gathered round, and tugged on his salt-and-pepper beard. There was a fierce light gleaming in his squinty eyes.

"And so we commend the body of Big Sam Gunnison to the earth, and his soul into the keeping of God Almighty. I knew Big Sam for thirty years. He never heard a single sermon I preached. He cussed like a cavalryman and drank rotgut like water. He killed six men that I know of, most of them no-account rustlers. Because of his adultery with a Mexican girl, his wife left him twenty years ago and took up with another man. I believe they are dead now. Big Sam outlived them both, for whatever that's worth.

"That Mexican girl, Maria Arista, lies here. And there's Sam's son, whom God saw fit to take from this world of sin and sorrow at a tender age, before he could be sullied. This is where Sam wanted to be laid to rest, and I suppose it is fitting, as this is the land he fought and bled for. Comanches, rustlers, bandits from the Bloody Border. He whipped them all. Some folks called Sam *mal hombre*. Maybe so. Maybe so. But he never told a lie, and he never failed to lend a helping hand to an honest man if the need arose. He would have given you the shirt off his back were you naked, and the food from his plate if you were hungry. He never mistreated an animal, unless it was a mule when the knobhead refused to budge, and he was always kind to children. So I believe that when the Lord measures Sam Gunnison's vices against his virtues He will in His infinite goodness and mercy see fit to grant our dear departed friend and neighbor admittance into His Kingdom. At least I will pray that it will be so, because I am still bound and determined to preach a sermon to Sam Gunnison, and it now appears that I will have to do it in the next life. Amen."

"Amen," echoed the congregation.

Reverend Gillum nodded to the cowboy gravediggers and then turned to a willow-slight, gray-headed woman who lingered by the grave as the rest of the people made for the horses and buggies and wagons further down the slope.

"If there is anything I can do for you, Mrs. Kenton . . ."

"No, thank you, Reverend."

The preacher nodded and moved on. Another man took his place. He was big, broad-shouldered, with a craggy face and steelcast eyes. Silver streaked his coal-black hair, brushed straight back from a widow's peak and curling at the shoulders.

"The reverend's offer goes double for me, ma'am."

She smiled and shook her head. "You've been very kind, Mr. Buckhorn. I can't thank you enough."

"No thanks are necessary, ma'am. Your brother and I didn't always see eye to eye, it's true. But I admired his grit and integrity. He was a hell of a man." His eyes flicked to the grave. "It won't be the same without him. But I don't see his daughter, Emmy . . ."

"No. She'll be heartbroken. But she had a long way to travel."

"When she arrives I'd like to call on her. Talk to her about her future plans."

"I can't speak for my niece, Mr. Buckhorn, but I would be very surprised were she to even consider selling the Rimfire."

"Well." Buckhorn shrugged, smiling faintly. "Maybe I can convince her. Make an offer she can't refuse."

"Perhaps. Now, if you'll excuse me . . . "

Buckhorn scanned the grim, sundark faces of the Rimfire riders standing a respectful distance behind Martha Kenton.

"I don't see Shell Harper, either."

She pointed, and Buckhorn looked further up the slope. At the crest of the ridge he saw three men on horseback, dark shapes against an angry sky.

Shell Harper felt sick and empty inside. He sat slumped in his three-quarter rig, strapped to the back of a lanky sorrel gelding he called Lucifer. A lean, wide-shouldered man with angular features, his piercing eyes were a deep bottle-green, and full of misery now as they gazed dismally down the slope at the grave beneath the trees, where the closest thing to a father he'd ever had was being put six feet under.

"Maybe we should mosey on down there, now that all those other folks are gone," suggested Addicks Bell.

Shell spared Addicks even a glance. The latter was trying to dry off his spectacles, a futile exercise in the midst of this fence-lifter.

"What for?" rasped Shell.

"Pay our last respects."

"I can pay them from here."

Addicks said no more. He glanced past Shell to the third rider, the slender *vaquero* named Joaquin Cruz. Joaquin had somehow managed to roll a quirly in this downpour, and now flicked a strike-anywhere to life with a thumbnail. The brief flare of the sulfur-tip illuminated a dark, aquiline, devilishly handsome face as Joaquin cupped the flame around the tip of the cigarette jutting from strong white teeth. Joaquin glanced at Addicks and just shrugged.

Addicks nodded. It was Shell Harper's call. Both he and Joaquin would stick with Shell, no matter how he wanted to handle this. After all, Shell had ridden for Rimfire a lot longer than either of them. Shell had been a young saddlebum of sixteen when Big Sam Gunnison took him in, a troubled youth angry at the world. Quite a handful by all accounts, but Sam had whipped him into shape, made a man out of him, and a tophand cowboy to boot. Now Shell was the Rimfire foreman, having come a long way from a wayward childhood on the mean streets of Hell's Half Acre, the bastard son of a two-dollar whore.

Wishing there was something he could say to ease his friend's pain, Addicks squinted downslope in what he presumed was the general direction of the grave—and sighed. He was nearly blind as a bat when it came to seeing things far-off. But trying to dry his see-betters was hopeless, so he hooked the specs to his ears.

He felt plenty bad about Sam Gunnison, too, but it was Shell who had gotten him this job. A few years back he had come to Texas, fleeing the drudgery of the family farm back in Illinois, wanting to be a cow-boy, with all the glamour that entailed. Well, it had turned out more hard work than glamour, but he wouldn't give it up for anything in the world.

It was Shell who had given him the chance, even though he'd known next to nothing about ranching or cattle or horses or . . . well, anything. And it was Shell who had stuck with him, and backed him up when some of the other hands ridiculed him. He'd borne the brunt of numerous pranks, but most of the time they had been in a good-natured vein—cowboys were inveterate practical jokers.

And on the occasions that there had been some pure-dee meanness behind the prank, Addicks had demonstrated to all concerned that while he wasn't much of a hand with sidegun or rifle, he had the hardest pair of fists in the county. Addicks was a rawboned youth, strong as an ox, due to his experience behind a middle-buster. In time the Rimfire outfit had accepted him, mostly because he never quit. Just didn't know the meaning of the word. He could rope and ride and brand with the rest of them now. And these days he could read his poetry without getting any smart remarks from his fellow denizens of the bunkhouse.

"I can't believe he's gone," muttered Shell.

"*Feo, fuerte, y valiente*," said Joaquin.

"What's that?" queried Addicks.

"He was ugly, strong, and brave. An *hombre del campo*."

Addicks nodded again. "Yeah. But looking at Sam Gunnison, I never figured he was mortal. Thought he'd be here forever, like the mountains, or the sky."

And yet, mused the Illinois farmboy turned Texican cowpoke, Sam Gunnison had died in a fall from a horse—he, who had lived his whole life on a mustang's hurricane deck. Life was full of ironies.

Addicks glanced sidelong at Shell again. Curious, the way the Rimfire foreman was acting. They'd put Big Sam in a quick-built coffin in one of the downstairs rooms of the main house, waiting for his only blood relatives—his sister, Martha Kenton, and daughter, Emmy—to arrive. At first the hands had been stunned and listless, having lost their boss, but Shell put them back to work with a vengeance, and worked them hard. Himself, too, and not once, far as Addicks knew, had he entered that downstairs room where Big Sam's mortal remains lay in rustic frontier state.

Martha Kenton lived in Waco, where she ran the mercantile which her deceased husband had established, and it took her only two days to reach the Rimfire range. But Emmy, Sam's daughter, lived in St. Louis, and that was a far piece, and they couldn't hold up the interment long enough for her to get here from there. Through it all, Shell had steered well clear of the coffin, as though death was contagious. So, mused Addicks, here they were, at the top of the ridge, two hundred yards away from Sam Gunnison's final resting place.

"There goes Mrs. Kenton and the rest of the outfit," said Joaquin, watching the buggy, driven by Martha Kenton, turn along the road connecting Lampasas and San Saba, trailed by the Rimfire riders. The whole crew, apart from a couple of line riders and the old cook, Lopez. In stating the obvious, the *vaquero* was implying that it might be time to move along and join the others for the return ride to the ranch.

"You two go on ahead," said Shell.

"What about you?" asked Addicks.

Shell almost told him to mind his own business. Almost, but not quite. "I think I'll go see what Moss Buckhorn is up to."

Alarm bells went off inside Addicks' head. Shell had never had a nice thing to say about Moss Buckhorn. If a Rimfire bridle strap broke, Shell suspected Buckhorn of having something to do with it.

So what did Shell have up his sleeve now? Whatever it was, Addicks didn't think he was going to like it. Usually an easy-going feller with a quick smile, Shell was the kind of *segundo* who got men to do what he told them because they respected him, not because they feared him. But lately he'd been driving the outfit hard, and he didn't smile anymore.

But rather than pry into Shell's intentions—which would be about as fruitless as trying to dry spectacles out in a frog-strangler—Addicks said, casual-like, "Reckon I'll ride along with you."

"Me, too," said Joaquin.

"No, you two go back with the others. I'll catch up."

"Look, Shell . . . " began Addicks.

"Do what I tell you or draw your pay," snapped the Rimfire foreman, and spurred Lucifer into a jumping-start gallop down the long slope.

Getting his spooked horse under control, Addicks said, "Wonder what's got into him? Reckon we ought to trail him, Joaquin?"

"No," said the laconic *vaquero*. "I like my job."

"Oh, he wouldn't fire us."

They angled their ponies across the slope, setting a course to intercept the buggy and line of riders on the San Saba Road.

When Moss Buckhorn reached the road he turned his horse east, towards Lampasas, in the opposite direction from that taken by Martha Kenton and the Rimfire outfit. The townsfolk who had ventured from town to attend Big Sam's funeral had all preceded him. The rain was coming down heavily now, and for that reason Shell Harper figured he could take the road too, and stay maybe a hundred yards behind Buckhorn. At that distance he could just barely see Buckhorn up ahead in the gray gloom. If Buckhorn looked behind him to check his backtrail he would spot Shell, but the Rimfire foreman figured that was okay. If worse came to worst he would flat-out lie and tell Buckhorn he was going into town on his own business.

He wasn't really sure why he was following Buckhorn in the first place. One thing was certain—Buckhorn wanted to get his greedy hands on the Rimfire. Always had wanted to. It had the best graze and the best water in this neck of the woods, and in that respect at least put Buckhorn's spread to shame, though Buckhorn's spread covered more territory. Putting the two ranches together would give Buckhorn an honest-to-God cattle kingdom that would rival Captain King's sagebrush empire down south.

But being a cattle baron wasn't all Buckhorn wanted out of life. No, he was the kind who wanted to own a piece of everything and everyone in sight. He owned the hotel in Lampasas, a half-interest in one of the saloons, and a mercantile. He was a partner in the Vallecito Freight Company.

Shell had an urge to just confront Buckhorn and tell him that hell would freeze over before he got the Rimfire. But then, that wasn't his decision. Emmy Gunnison owned the ranch now, right down to the last horseshoe nail.

The thought of Emmy gave Shell Harper a funny feeling in his chest. When he'd first come to the Rimfire, Emmy had been a thirteen-year-old tomboy, who could ride and shoot as well as any of the hired hands. Though she dressed like a man and sometimes cussed like a man and even kept her chestnut hair cut short like a man, Shell had never mistaken her for anything but female. In fact, looking back on it now, Shell decided he'd been attracted to Emmy almost from the start. For sure he had missed her when, after a falling out with her father—nobody knew what it was about—she'd gone to stay with her Aunt Martha. Shell had later heard that she'd married a man named Stegall, and moved to St. Louis. Stegall, a West Point graduate and veteran of the late War Between the States, had resigned his commission after Appomattox and become a civil engineer. That was all Shell knew about him, other than that he was dead, killed when a Mississippi River sternwheeler exploded and sank.

Now Emmy was coming home.

Shell figured Moss Buckhorn would exert all the pressure he could on Emmy to get her to sell the Rimfire to him. *And if she does, what will I do?* wondered Shell. The possibility made him cold inside. The Rimfire was the only home he'd ever known. Would Emmy want to keep it? Running a ranch was a big job. Her roots were here, but she had neatly severed all ties with her father and the spread. After all these years in St. Louis, maybe she wouldn't want to live in the *brasada* country again.

As they drew nearer to Lampasas Shell expected Buckhorn to veer off to the north, toward his ranch. Instead, he rode straight on into town.

Lampasas looked deserted. Buttery lamplight poured from a few of the windows, but not a single living soul, not even a stray dog, was brave enough to venture out into the red quagmires of the street.

Buckhorn dismounted in front of the Bulldog Saloon, tethered his horse next to a dappled gray, and climbed up onto the boardwalk, passing through the open door of the watering hole and out of Shell's sight.

So he's come to town for a drink to cut the chill, thought Shell. *Maybe I should join him. But what would I say? You won't get Rimfire if I have anything to do with it, Moss Buckhorn. What would he say in reply? Probably laugh. Thing is, I* don't *have anything to do with it. It would be empty talk, and we'd both know it.*

Shell steered his horse to a hitching post in front of Goetzmann the bootmaker's shop, tied up there, and walked along the boardwalk fronting the clapboards and adobes on the north side of Front Street, until he had arrived at Barthell's mercantile, almost directly across the town's main thoroughfare from the Bulldog. He could see the entire length of the saloon from this vantage point, through the open door and the plate-glass window.

Buckhorn was at the bar. The apron, Leon, stood across from him, pouring whiskey into a shotglass. Leon spoke. Buckhorn nodded, knocked the drink back, and shook his head when Leon lifted the bottle an inch off the mahogany, asking without words if Buckhorn desired a refill. Instead, Buckhorn put a piece of hard money on the bar and walked out.

Shell backed up into the recessed doorway of Barthell's she-bang and pulled his hatbrim down low over his face.

But Buckhorn didn't look in his direction, glancing instead over his shoulder, through the plate-glass window. At a table just inside the window sat a black-bearded man in a gray longcoat. Shell had never seen him before. He could see the man clearly, in profile, directly beneath the arched letters, SALOON, stenciled in fancy red and gold script on the glass. The man glanced out the window. His gaze connected with Buckhorn's. Shell thought he detected a nod, an almost imperceptible tilt of the head. Buckhorn moved on as the man rose from the table. He didn't go to his horse, but walked east along the boardwalk. The man in the gray longcoat emerged from the Bulldog and followed in his wake, about twenty paces back.

Shell's heartbeat jumped from a walk to a canter. Something was smelling mighty rotten all of a sudden. Clearly Buckhorn had come to town to meet this stranger. Just as clearly he did not want the meeting to occur in a public place, among witnesses.

"Shell! What can I do you out of?"

The Rimfire foreman whirled, startled. Barthell had come up behind him, a beefy, jovial man wearing a long canvas apron and carrying a dripping mop.

"Come on in," boomed the storekeeper. "But watch your step. Damned roof leaks like a sieve."

Shell grabbed two handfuls of apron and shirt and manhandled Barthell back into the store. The shopkeeper uttered a strangled sound, being a man unaccustomed to physical violence, and caught completely by surprise. Once inside the she-bang proper, Shell released him. Barthell immediately began to wax indignant.

"Look here, Shell! What's the meaning . . . ?"

But Shell had turned away, to peer through the store window. Had the attention of either Buckhorn or the stranger in the long, gray coat been drawn to the mercantile doorway by Barthell's bullhorn voice? A drum roll of thunder shook the window glass in its frame. Both Buckhorn and the stranger were still walking. Neither one was looking back towards Barthell's establishment. Shell released pent-up breath.

"I demand to know what's going on," insisted Barthell, his ego bruised.

"Sorry, Mike. I'll have to explain later."

With that Shell was gone, hurrying along the boardwalk on the north side of the street, sloshing through the muck at the mouths of the alleys, about fifty feet behind the stranger who was still following Buckhorn at twenty paces on the other side. *If they look around they'll see me for sure*, thought Shell. Then what would they do? Shell had no idea, but he felt he had to take the chance.

Buckhorn was up to no good, and Shell's hunch was that it had something to do with the Rimfire.

Stopping at the door to the office of the Vallecito Freight Company, Buckhorn finally did look around, first to ascertain whether the stranger was still behind him, and then to check the street. Shell managed to duck down a convenient alley and avoid detection. Peering around the corner of Koehler's barber shop, he saw Buckhorn unlock the office door, push it open, and wait to allow the stranger to enter before him. With one last scan of the rain-pounded street, Buckhorn followed, shutting the door behind him. Lamplight leaked through the wooden shutters on the windows.

Shell pondered his next move. He had come this far—he had to find out what Moss Buckhorn had up his sleeve. But how was he going to go about doing that?

Slogging across the muddy street, the Rimfire foreman reached the corner of the freight company office building. He could see absolutely nothing through the shuttered front windows, so he avoided the boardwalk fronting the clapboard structure, for fear that a loose board would betray him, and moved instead down a narrow alley between the office and Doc Webb's. Rounding the back corner of the freight office he pulled up short, glimpsing movement in the rear window. It was Buckhorn, pulling down a canvas shade.

Putting his ear to the clapboard wall, Shell could dimly hear voices from within, but they were too muffled to tell what was being said, so he grit his teeth and went around the corner again, to crouch beneath the window.

"What kind of problem?"

This was Buckhorn. The shade was not down all the way; through a half-inch slit Shell could see Buckhorn sitting in a chair behind a kneehole desk, his back to the window. He heard a slow measured thumping sound that puzzled him for an instant—then he saw the stranger in the gray longcoat move across the room in front of the desk, and back again. He was pacing the room.

"I don't kill women, as a rule."

Buckhorn drawled, "I don't recall saying anything in the telegram about killing a woman."

"I'm not stupid, Mr. Buckhorn."

"I know that, Mr. Pratt. If you were, I wouldn't have sent for you."

"If I was, I'd be dead."

"I suppose so, in your line of work."

"I've heard them talking down at the saloon. About how Sam Gunnison's dead as last Sunday's dinner, and his daughter is inheriting the Rimfire Ranch. They also talk about how you want that spread all for yourself, and what you might try to get your hands on it."

"Is that so?"

"That's so. Yeah. Now you send for me. A . . . troubleshooter. I take care of other's folk's problems. Sometimes requires a little gunplay. I never got much in the way of proper schoolin', but I can put two and two together as well as the next man. It's Gunnison's daughter you want out of the way. Has to be so."

Shell's blood ran cold. He had suspected Buckhorn of planning some form of mischief, but now that his suspicions were confirmed, he could scarcely believe it.

"I don't want her killed, Mr. Pratt," sighed Buckhorn. "But I do want her out of the way, yes. I want you to get her before she arrives. Then I want you to take her somewhere and hold her there long enough for them to figure she's dead. Then I'll have the Rimfire. Hell, she couldn't handle a spread like that anyway. Sam Gunnison did, with grit and gunpowder. But now he's gone under. . . ."

3

"How long you want her to disappear for?" asked Pratt.

"Let's say three months. By then they'll be sure she's dead."

Pratt was silent a moment, still pacing up and down. "For someone like Sam Gunnison's daughter they'll put on one hell of a search."

"Oh, yes, they'll search high and low. They'll turn all of Texas up by her heels and give her a hard shake. Which is why I need someone like you, Mr. Pratt. You've been both hunter and hunted in the course of your career."

"Why don't you want her dead?"

"I'm not a murderer. Would you care for a drink?" Buckhorn opened a drawer and brandished a bottle of Old Overshoe.

"Don't mind if I do." As Buckhorn brought two glasses from the drawer and filled them with the amber whiskey, Pratt said, "You'll have trouble when I let her loose. She'll figure you were behind it."

"She'll have no proof. You'll be long gone. And of course you will never mention my name in her presence."

"'Course not. Thanks."

There was a lull in the conversation as both men slugged back the nerve medicine.

"But folks would naturally wonder why she'd been kidnapped," remarked Pratt, sounding a little breathless from the whiskey.

"By all accounts, Emmy Gunnison is a very pretty young woman."

Again Pratt fell silent, as the full implications of Buckhorn's comment sank in.

"Are you tellin' me . . . ?"

"I'm saying you're a man and she's a woman. A quite desirable woman."

"Christ," said Pratt. "They'd hang me for certain if they caught me."

"But they won't catch you, will they, Mr. Pratt?"

Pratt grunted. "Well, if I'm gonna be accused of the crime I might as well do the deed. But I'll need more than that to get me to take this job."

"Naturally."

"I'll never be able to show my face in this part of the country again. Hell, I'll have to stay north of the Platte, at least. Maybe Canada."

"Or Mexico."

"Don't cotton to Mexico, myself."

"How does five thousand dollars strike you?"

Pratt let loose a low whistle. "There's a handsome wage."

"The wages of sin are always handsome, aren't they? And, as a bonus, you'll be sinning with Emmy Gunnison for three months."

"You got yourself a deal. Where is she now?"

Shell thought, *I'll bust in there right now and haul them both straight over to Sheriff Dunn.* He felt the reassuring weight of the holstered Remington Army beneath his slicker.

"Hey you!"

Unbeknownst to Shell, a man had emerged through the gate to the Vallecito wagon yard, adjacent to the freight office, a compound encompassed by an adobe wall, and containing a forge, storage shed, yardmaster's office, and corrals for mules and horses. The main gate opened onto Front Street, but this side gate permitted easy access to the back door of the freight office.

The man rushed at Shell, whose first instinct was to run. All of a sudden it was three against one, he'd lost the element of surprise, and he didn't want to be recognized if he could manage to get away. Instead, he lowered his head and bulled straight into the other's charge.

They went down in a tangle. The man flipped Shell over his shoulder. They both leapt to their feet, covered with mud, but Shell came up with his hands full of the stuff, which he hurled into his adversary's face. Then he charged again, landing a punch on the man's jawbone. The man crumpled. Shell lost his footing and fell on top of him and punched him again, knocking him out.

Out of an eye-corner Shell saw the shade on the back window of the freight office go up. Mustard lamplight spilled out into the nightlike gloom. Shell snatched his hat out of the mud and scurried away. Running for all he was worth, he circled the Vallecito wagon yard before turning up to Front Street. Seeing that the street was quiet, and that there was no one in front of the freight office, he judged it safe to hurry across to Lucifer, tethered in front of the bootmaker's shop. Hauling himself into the saddle, he rode out of Lampasas.

"So you were right about Moss Buckhorn," mused Addicks.

Shell simply nodded. He, Joaquin, and Addicks stood on the porch of the Rimfire bunkhouse. The rain had stopped shortly after sundown, and now he could glimpse a few stars through the wind-shredded clouds.

"So what are we going to do about it?" asked Addicks.

"I say we go into town and fill *Señor* Buckhorn full of lead," suggested Joaquin.

Addicks gawked at the *vaquero*, who was leaning nonchalantly against the bunkhouse wall, rolling a cigarette. That the usually easygoing Joaquin could make such a suggestion was startling enough. But the offhanded way in which he made it, as casually as one might suggest going into town to have a drink at the Bulldog, sent a shiver down Addicks Bell's spine. There was obviously more to Joaquin Cruz than met the eye. Beneath that live-and-let-live facade lurked something rattlesnake-cold and deadly.

"That's cold-blooded murder, Joaquin."

Joaquin just shrugged. "He deserves it."

"And we'd all stretch hemp," said Shell.

They lapsed into silence. What Moss Buckhorn had in mind for Emmy Gunnison had stunned Addicks and Joaquin. Just flat out killing her would be better than the scheme he had devised. Addicks, for one, figured he had never heard anything so downright despicable in his whole life. Even the roughest hombre on the frontier treated a woman with respect.

"You think they recognized you, Shell?" he asked.

"I don't think so. I'm fairly certain the man who came at me never got a good look at my face. As for Buckhorn . . . " Shell thought back, replaying the scene in his mind, and shook his head. Buckhorn had been in a well-lighted room looking out into storm-swept darkness. "No, I don't reckon he knew me."

"But he knew someone was listening in on his palaver with that man Pratt," said Addicks. "So maybe he'll get cold feet and call the whole thing off."

"Maybe. But I doubt it. Too much at stake. And we can't take the chance." Shell drew a long breath, silently cursed himself. "I shouldn't have run. I should've busted in there and taken both Buckhorn and that sonuvabitch Pratt to the calabozo, under the gun."

"You'd have wound up with your toes curled,

most likely," said Addicks. "But you could still go to the sheriff."

"Dunn would never find Pratt now. It would be my word against Buckhorn's. Who would he believe? Pratt was my evidence. Anybody could see he's a hardcase. A hired gun."

"Guess you're right. So what do we do?"

"I've got to get to Emmy before Pratt does."

"You mean *we've* got to."

"No. I want you two to stay here and take care of things while I'm gone."

"I don't like the idea of you going up against Pratt alone. You said it yourself. He's a hired gun. With Joaquin and me along the odds are on your side."

"You never knew Emmy, Add. She's a crack shot. She and I can handle Pratt. You'll have your hands full with problems here."

Addicks knew what Shell was referring to. In the past month or so, a gang of nightriders had been making off with Rimfire stock.

"You going to tell *Señora* Kenton?" queried Joaquin.

Shell looked across the hardpack at the big house. It looked more like a fortress than a home—a square adobe structure, built around a courtyard and enclosing a well. The walls, three feet thick, were impervious to fire and bullet. They had withstood Comanche attacks and bandit raids. The shutters on the long narrow windows were crosshatched with gun slots. There was a big gate in back so that the cavallard could be driven into the safety of the courtyard if the need arose.

"Reckon not," said the Rimfire foreman. "Come morning, you can tell her I've gone to meet Emmy. She doesn't need to know the rest."

They turned in. Shell was up a couple of hours before sunrise, having been unable to sleep a wink. He slipped out of the bunkhouse with rifle and war bag without waking any of the hands—or so he thought. At the horse pen he whistled up Lucifer, and was in the process of cinching his rig to the pony's backside when Addicks Bell appeared.

"Doesn't feel right, letting you go alone," admitted Addicks.

"You fret like an old mother hen, plowpusher," said Shell, with a mitigating smile.

"Without me and Joaquin to look out for you, you'll end up buzzard bait."

"Just try to remember which side of a horse to get up on while I'm not here to wet-nurse you."

Addicks grinned, but the grin was short-lived. "If you and Emmy don't come back, you reckon Mrs. Kenton will sell out to Buckhorn?"

"She's got no stake in the Rimfire."

"Then you just better come back."

"I know. If I didn't, you'd be out of a job. No other outfit would take you on."

"You taught me everything I know—so you're probably right."

Shell gave the latigo one last tug, tied it up over the rigging ring, dropped the saddle fender and turned to stick out his hand. Addicks shook it.

"Keep Joaquin from going after Moss Buckhorn," said Shell.

"It doesn't seem right somehow, letting Buckhorn off scot-free."

"His day'll come."

"How are you going to find Emmy?"

"She'll come down from Fort Worth on the stage. All I have to do is ride up the line until we meet."

Which is exactly what Pratt will do, thought Addicks. But he didn't say it. Didn't need to. It was the thought foremost on Shell's mind.

Shell climbed aboard Lucifer, gave his friend a curt nod, and rode away.

4

Her given name was Mary, but everyone knew her better as The Widow. The Widow Stanton, they called her. Most of the other fourteen people who resided in Spanish Station did not even remember her other name. They thought calling her The Widow suited her because she had spurned several suitors in the years following her husband's demise. She seemed to like being a widow woman.

It was the Widow Stanton who first saw him coming into town. Wiping dough-covered hands on her red-and-white checkered apron, peering out of her kitchen window, she gave the stranger a long, hard look and figured him for trouble.

He was afoot, leading a lamed horse, up the road through the mesquite flats. He could be on the dodge, she thought, and ran his cayuse into the ground. Or maybe he had run afoul of Comanches. This was the time of the Yellow Moon, the time the Comanches preferred for raiding. And if the Comanches were on the rampage, well, that was about the worst trouble of all.

For another thing, the man looked lean and mean, like a loafer wolf. The Widow Stanton was a bona fide pioneer woman. She'd spent a quarter of century on the Texas frontier, and she had seen all kinds of men. And men like this one you tried to keep from crossing.

She passed through the cool dimness of the dining room into the front hall of the clapboard Victorian on the edge of town, and from there into the bright shade of the veranda, as the man trudged across a yard spotted with alders. She could not see his face. His head was down, a sweat-stained hatbrim concealed all of his features except a beard-stubbled chin. He came straight on to the porch steps before stopping and lifting his head.

"Howdy," she said.

Something like a smile touched the taut corners of Shell Harper's mouth. He could tell she was unafraid of him, and he admired her for that, because he figured he looked like hell warmed over. She was a wide-hipped, heavy-set woman. Her dress was plain, faded gingham. Her face was strong, compassionate, deeply etched by the vicissitudes of pioneer life. She smelled of starch and lye, a good, clean smell.

"Howdy," he replied, a parched whisper.

"Passing through?"

"Looking for the southbound stage."

"You come from the south."

"Yep."

"The southbound ought to roll in 'bout sundown. Big storm a few days ago washed out the bridge over the Brazos. Held the stage up."

"You seen a man the last day or two? Black beard, wears a gray longcoat?"

She shook her head. "Can't say as I have. What's amiss with that pony?"

"Cholla."

"Take it yonder to the station yard. Have Jesus look at it. He'll fix it up with one of his potions. Tell him I sent you over. Widow Stanton, that's me. And you'd be . . . ?"

"Shell Harper. I ride for the Rimfire, down Lampasas way."

She had already noted that not once had he looked over his shoulder. So he wasn't too worried about his backtrail. Meant that, like as not, he wasn't wanted.

"Meeting somebody on the stage?" It was the only scenario that made any sense—he had come from the south looking to meet the southbound stage.

He nodded. "Does it lay over here for the night?"

"And rolls out the next morning."

"Reckon I'll need a room, then."

"Clean room is four bits, and two home-cooked meals thrown in for good measure. There's a warm spring that comes up out of the ground behind the four-holer, if you're of a mind to wash off half of Texas."

He nodded in the direction of the pump and trough nearer at hand. "That'll do, if you can spare the water."

"Have at it. Well ain't given out in twenty-five years, so I reckon it won't today."

She watched him as he pumped up fresh well water. Sweeping off his hat, he put his head under the torrent gushing from the iron spout. The Widow Stanton wanted to know more about this man. Who was the bearded character in the longcoat he had asked about? Who was he hoping to meet up with on the southbound stage from Fort Worth? He hadn't run afoul of Comanches, and he wasn't on the dodge, but that didn't mean he wasn't bringing trouble with him.

But you had to be careful out here with the questions you asked. It was poor frontier etiquette to pry too much. A person did well to mind his or her own business.

Straightening to shake like a dog coming out of a creek, Shell took a long look at the town of Spanish Station, which amounted to seven buildings on a wide

rutted street about a good, long stone's throw in
length. There was, in addition to the widow woman's
house, a saloon, a general store, the stage station with
adjoining livery and smitty, and three houses at the
other end of the street that appeared to be private
dwellings. Spanish Station existed because of its
springs—there was plenty of water year-round—and
because it lay about halfway between Fort Worth and
Waco—or, as a Texas range rider would say, "Hell's
Half Acre" and "Six-shooter Junction." It was a good
spot for a stageline station, and also serviced the cowboys who worked nearby spreads.

They called it Spanish Station because the first
white man to settle here—the Widow Stanton's husband—had discovered the bleached bones of a long-
ago-massacred detail of Spanish troops. Legend had it
that the detail was on the way from one *presidio* to
another when, having camped for the night at these
springs, it was attacked by a large party of hostile
Indians.

Shell didn't think it likely that Pratt had managed
to come into town unseen by the Widow Stanton. She
struck him as the type who made it her business to
know everybody's comings and goings. But just in
case, he decided to check at the general store and the
saloon.

Depositing his saddle and war bag on the Widow
Stanton's porch, he took Lucifer across to the stage station and found the hostler named Jesus, a wizened old
Mexican who said little but whose eyes harbored the
wisdom of the ages. He examined the swollen postern
and then nodded when Shell asked him if he could
mend the horse. How long would it take before Lucifer
was good as new? Jesus held up three fingers. Shell figured he would have to make arrangements with the
widow woman to hire someone who could bring the
horse at least part of the way back to Rimfire. It was his
intention to join Emmy on the stage.

His next stop was the general store. To his surprise he found it closed up, so he crossed the street to the saloon.

There were two horses hitched to the post in front of the watering hole. They both carried a Slash B brand. Shell remembered that a dappled gray had been tethered at the Bulldog Saloon in Lampasas when Buckhorn had entered that establishment to make contact with Pratt. Was the gray Pratt's pony? Seemed likely.

Stepping into the saloon, Shell paused to let his eyes adjust to the dimness of the interior. A man stood behind the bar, reading a dog-eared Wide-Awake novel. Three men sat at a deal table. Two of them were obviously range riders, by their garb. The third man was dressed in a brown broadcloth suit. He had a narrow sallow face with dark soulful eyes and thick black mustache completely hiding his mouth. He was shuffling a deck of No. 220 Steamboat pasteboards. His nimble fingers were long and pale and the nails were well manicured. Those black eyes flicked towards Shell.

"Try your luck?" he asked.

"No, thanks." Shell crossed to the bar.

"Name your poison," said the apron.

Shell ordered a shot of whiskey. As the bar dog poured, the Rimfire foreman asked if he had seen a man with a black beard who wore a gray longcoat.

"Cain't say that I have."

Shell downed the bravemaker.

"Store across the street's closed," he observed.

"You need any possibles, mosey on down to the house at the end of the street, the one with the 'dobe wall around it. That's Ike Cosper's place. He owns the store. He don't usually open her up less he's got some business."

Thanking the bartender, Shell left the saloon. He paused in the boardwalk shade and scanned the raw-edged structures lining Spanish Station's sorry excuse for a street as the whiskey made a warm explosion in his belly. Then he headed for the south end of town. He was feeling better about Pratt. Either he had beaten Buckhorn's hired gun here, or Pratt had decided against taking the job after all. But Shell wanted to be thorough, so he made up his mind to have a word with Ike Cosper.

Reaching Cosper's house, Shell stepped over the low, crumbling adobe wall that encircled the storekeeper's property. At first he did not see the man leaning against the fieldstone wall of a smokehouse located in the back corner of the enclosure. But as Shell stepped toward the house the man straightened—one fast fluid motion—and sunlight glimmered on gunmetal.

Startled, Shell halted in his tracks.

"I didn't see you standing there," he said lamely.

"I saw you."

The rifle was a Henry repeater, and it wasn't pointed at anything in particular, cradled conveniently in the man's arms. The man's voice was hard and unemotional. Like the man himself, mused Shell. He wore a dun-colored duster, heavy twill pants thrust into mule-ear boots. His face was square-cut, rugged, with a drooping sandy-red mustache framing a thin mouth.

"Didn't mean to disturb you," said Shell.

"No bother."

"I'm looking for Ike Cosper."

"He rolled out in a wagon about an hour ago. Delivering goods to a spread near here."

Shell nodded. "Much obliged."

The man nodded once. Shell went back over the adobe wall. He didn't look back until he had reached the shade of the boardwalk fronting the saloon. From this vantage point he could see over the low wall with a good view of the smokehouse. He watched as the man in the duster removed a padlock from the smokehouse door. Opening the door, he took two long steps back and leveled the Henry. A slender young man emerged. Hatless, his lank yellow hair hung down in his eyes. His white muslin shirt and whipcord pants were soiled and torn. He stretched like a just-awakened parlor cat.

Again sunlight glimmered—this time off the manacles on the man's wrists.

5

Shell walked back to the Stanton house. The widow woman told him that supper would be on the table in an hour. She'd brought some fresh water for the wash-basin, which sat on a long table on the side porch, and a clean towel besides. A razor and bar of lye soap were also provided. "In case you want to come to table look-ing respectable," she said.

"Yes, ma'am," said Shell, who could take a hint as well as the next man.

He scraped the stubble off his lean, hard cheeks, splashed cold water on his face and groped for the towel. Hearing bootheels on the floor planks he had a bad moment, thinking of Pratt, and squinched an eye open and recognized the gambler.

"Game over?"

"They ran out of money."

"A month to earn it, a day to spend it."

The gambler smiled. "You a preacher?"

"Not preaching. Just saying they work hard for their pay."

"I work hard taking it from them. You a cowboy?"

"Yeah. But I don't play cards."

The gambler shrugged, looked Spanish Station over, and grimaced.

"I think it's time I started looking for greener pastures."

Shell knew the type. They rode the stagelines, laying over in a town for a spell, giving foolish cowboys the opportunity to try their luck, always moving on eventually, because a cowboy once burned was twice shy. Shell didn't see any artillery, but he figured the man was heeled, because occasionally a busted range rider was known to get ugly about losing his poke, especially when he'd swallowed too much rotgut.

"This is a community with no prospects and precious few redeeming virtues," said the gambler. "One of those virtues happens to be the widow woman's cooking." He sniffed the air.

Shell dumped the soapy water of the basin over the edge of the porch. He saw two men crossing the street, quartering for the livery. The one wearing the irons was in the lead. The tall grim character in the duster followed, Henry rifle cradled in his arm. Shell could hear the big man's Mexican spurs sing as they scuffed the rutted hardpack of the street.

"Know who that is?" asked the gambler.

"Never seen either one of 'em before today."

"The big galoot is a Texas Ranger, no less. Jack Ember. They say he cleaned out the Massey Gang single-handed."

"One fight, one man," said Shell.

"Yes, that's the Ranger motto, isn't it? Ember's a cold-eyed killer. I saw him gun down the Chireno Kid in King Fisher's Blue Wing a couple years ago. That's Billy Bishop wearing the outlaw jewelry."

"Billy Bishop. The road agent?"

"The one and only."

"Thank God for that."

"They say he's gunned down a dozen men. But I reckon his killing and robbing days are over. Ranger Ember is hauling him back to Austin to stand trial. He'll be guest of honor at a necktie social."

Shell squinted at the gambler. "You know a lot."

"Cowboys talk a lot. Name's Luther Killough."

"Shell Harper."

They shook hands. Shell was surprised at how soft Killough's hands were.

"Passing through?" asked the gambler.

"Waiting on the stage."

"Then I guess we'll be traveling companions for a ways." Killough nodded at the Texas Ranger and his prisoner as they disappeared into the livery. "All of us. Since Bishop's gang is still on the prowl, I guess the Ranger figures he'll have a better chance of getting Billy to Austin by stage."

"Well," said Shell, ready to change the subject. "I brought along a clean shirt. Reckon now's the time to wear it."

"I'm sure the widow woman would appreciate that."

Shell's rig and war bag were still on the porch where he'd left them, so he carried them inside. Widow Stanton told him to take the room at the top of the stairs. The room was comfortably appointed. He admired the chintz curtains on the window that offered a view through the tops of the alders at the mesquite flats, and the quilted counterpane on the bed caught his eye too. Digging his spare shirt out of the war bag, he shook it out and changed. Then he thought about the Remington on his hip. He didn't think the Widow Stanton would take too kindly to his coming to table armed, but since he had no idea if or when Pratt might show up, he was loathe to leave the sidegun in his room. So he decided to take his chances and keep the shooting iron strapped on.

He heard, very faintly, the sound of the stage coming in, and rushed to the window. There it was, kicking up a plume of dust.

Emmy!

Shell's heart began to hammer against his ribcage.

All of a sudden his throat was desert dry. So many years had passed since last he had set eyes on Emmy Gunnison. Would she even remember him? Probably not. But *he* still remembered. Especially remembered how bad he'd felt the day she left Rimfire.

Suddenly and inexplicably scared, Shell steeled himself and turned for the door, gathering up his hat.

As he emerged from his room a young man wearing a serape collided with him at the top of the stairs. The impact threw Shell off balance, all but spilling him down the staircase. Reacting by reflex, Shell braced himself against the wall and, dropping a shoulder, slammed the young man against the banister.

A flash of violent temper twisted the young man's face. His hand swept the serape aside and dropped to the Starr Colt revolver on his hip. He only managed to halfway clear leather. Then he became very still, staring down the barrel of Shell's Remington.

"Don't ordinarily draw iron and not use it," rasped Shell. "But I plain dislike shooting somebody right before I sit down to grub. Sometimes it puts me off my feed."

For one long breathless moment the young man tottered precariously on the brink of a big mistake. But Shell's fierce calm shook the gun-happy youth loose from what little confidence he had in his own abilities. His nerve broke. He let go of the Starr. It slipped back into its oiled holster. Flushing, he sneered, "Why don't you watch where you're going? Knock me down the stairs next time."

"I'll give it some thought," replied Shell, and leathered the Remington.

Prudent enough not to take offense, the young man brushed past Shell and proceeded down the stairs. "Smart hombres who like breathing stay out of my way," he muttered truculently without looking Shell square in the eye.

Exhibiting prudence of his own, Shell let him

have the last word. He'd seen this kind before. Hardly old enough to require whisker-scraping, they wore big guns and talked big talk and carried a big chip on both shoulders. They often died young. As a rule they were unstable, unpredictable, and, as a result, sometimes dangerous out of all proportion to their talent.

Shell realized that he had been a lot like this youth in his younger days, before Sam Gunnison had set him straight. He'd never fancied himself a gunslick, but he'd been plenty mad at the whole world, always spoiling for a fight, and capable enough with a charcoal burner to keep folks' attention.

With some remorse he wondered if Emmy—if she remembered him at all—would remember him that way.

Negotiating the stairs, Shell stepped out onto the front porch. The Widow Stanton was there, shading her eyes as she watched the stagecoach roll in. The sun was casting long slanted shadows now. The young man with the Starr Colt under that ragged serape was there too. He glowered at Shell and moved on down the porch a ways. Killough, the gambler, was leaning nonchalantly against the house at the far end, meticulously cleaning his fingernails with a clasp knife's blade tip.

The jehu climbed the ribbons and brought the coach to a stop in front of the station across the street. He was a hefty gent wearing a fringed buckskin shirt and a forage cap pushed back on the top of a shaved head. The hostler, Jesus, came out of the livery to nod at him and take hold of the nearside leader in the six-horse hitch. The reinsman waved at the Widow Stanton and jumped nimbly out of the box to yank open the coach door.

The first passenger to emerge was a short, paunchy man in dusty tweed, carrying a big case that was almost too heavy for him. He started across the hardpack, lugging the case, and by the time he had taken ten steps his beet-red face was dripping perspiration.

And then Emmy climbed out of the coach.

She looked a whole lot different than Shell remembered. Instead of jeans and a man's work shirt—what amounted to a uniform in her younger years—she was wearing a blue serge traveling suit and white *camisa* with a bow at the neck. Her lustrous chestnut hair wasn't bobbed short, the way it used to be, but had grown long and was now bound up in a French braid. The jehu helped her down and then walked around to the boot and unstrapped the leather flaps to get at the luggage. Emmy looked around her at Spanish Station. His heart firmly lodged in his throat, Shell told himself he needed to mosey on out there to her. But while he thought about it, Killough acted.

"Where are you going?" asked Shell.

"Why, to welcome the little lady to Spanish Station," replied the gambler. "What any gentleman would do."

Shell got his feet unrooted from the porch planks and took long strides to overtake Killough. In passing, he told the gambler, "She's with me from now on."

Emmy was watching the jehu extract two large valises from the boot, and glanced at Shell as he drew near. The light of recognition dawned in the most beautiful blue eyes the Rimfire foreman had ever seen.

"Shell? Is that really you?"

"Emmy. You're . . . you're . . . "

Laughing, she gave him a hug. Shell felt his cheeks burning. Then, holding him at arm's length, she looked him over from heel to hatbrim.

"Shell, you're looking good."

"So are you, Emmy. Pretty as a prairie sunset."

"It's so good to see a familiar face. But what are you doing here?"

"Come to meet you."

Her face lost some of its glow. "Have they . . . buried Father?"

He nodded.

"I was afraid of that. The rains held us up."

"I'm sorry, Emmy."

She squeezed his arm and put on a brave smile. "No matter."

He stared, bewitched by her beauty, and only belatedly realized that he was staring, and blushed.

"It was good of you to come this far to meet me."

Suddenly tongue-tied, he shrugged. He wanted to tell her he would have ridden to Connecticut to meet her—wherever that was. And he wondered if he ought to tell her *why* he was here. But the reinsman was handing him the valises.

"There's your gear, miss," he said. "Yonder's the Stanton place. Should find a room there. We'll be rollin' out come daybreak."

"Thank you, Mr. O'Hara."

"My pleasure, ma'am."

She started for the house and Shell followed.

He would have to wait till later to tell her about Pratt, and the fate Moss Buckhorn had planned for her.

6

The Widow Stanton had only three rooms to let. The gambler, Killough, was in one of them, and the youth who thought himself a gunslinger had another. Shell's was the third. He gave it to Emmy. The youth, whose name was Grissom, remarked with a leer that he wouldn't mind sharing his quarters with the lady, at which point Shell would have beat him to a bloody pulp but for the look Emmy gave him.

That left the other passenger, who introduced himself as Horace Teague, without a room, but he assured the widow woman that he would be quite content to sleep on the rug in the downstairs parlor, since neither Grissom nor Killough offered to share their accommodations. Teague announced that he was a whiskey salesman, a purveyor of genuine Kentucky bourbon, the best sipping whiskey in the world, and went off to the saloon to see if he could persuade the owner of that establishment to place an order.

Shell carried Emmy's bags up to the room and moved his saddle and war bag out into the upstairs hall. Then he went back down to find Emmy. She was on the side porch, washing her face and hands in the basin. Grissom was there, leaning against the house, and he hadn't lost that leer yet.

"Get lost," said Shell.

"I was just talkin' to the lady."

"She doesn't want to talk to you."

"It doesn't matter, Shell," said Emmy.

"We're just gettin' acquainted is all," said Grissom. "Seein' as how we're gonna be travelin' together for a spell."

"Git," said Shell. "I'm not going to tell you again."

Grissom pushed away from the wall, a scowl on his face, thumbs hooked under his gunbelt, and adopted a calculated pose. "You're askin' for it, cowboy."

Shell hit him.

The Rimfire foreman's fist caught Grissom cleanly on the chin. The gun-hung youth toppled off the side porch and landed flat on his back. Wheezing, he rolled over and got up on hands and knees, dazed, drooling blood. Then he groped for the Starr revolver. Shell was waiting for that. As soon as the gun cleared leather he kicked it out of Grissom's grasp. Grabbing a handful of serape, Shell hauled the kid to his feet.

"She's with me," rasped Shell. "So I don't want you talking to her. Savvy? In fact, I don't want to catch you even looking at her." He gave Grissom a vigorous shake. "Are you listening?"

"Yeah," mumbled Grissom. "I hear you."

"Good." Shell gave him a shove. Grissom tripped over his feet and sprawled in the dust again. Picking himself up, he stumbled to his gun and picked it up. He threw a glance at Shell. Shell was waiting, his hand hovering near the Remington on his hip. Grissom flirted with the idea, then thought better of it. Holstering the Starr, he disappeared around the corner of the house.

Shell turned to find a look of stern disapproval on Emmy's face.

"I see you haven't changed much," she said.

The words cut him deep.

"He's nothing but trouble, Emmy."

"I can take care of myself, Shell."

"I know that. But . . . "

"But what? I don't need a bodyguard."

"Yes, you do."

She just looked at him, a furrow forming above the bridge of her nose. "Why do you say that?"

Shell drew long breath. "It's Moss Buckhorn, Emmy. He's bought himself a hard case named Pratt."

"So? What's that got to do with me?"

"Everything. Buckhorn wants the Rimfire."

"He always has."

"He figures with you out of the way he'll stand a real good chance of getting it."

"Buckhorn hired a man to kill me?"

"Not exactly. This feller Pratt's been paid to kidnap you. Keep you under wraps for a spell. Long enough for everybody to figure you're dead."

It took a moment for Emmy to digest all the implications of this news. "How do you know all this, Shell?"

"It's a long story. I heard 'em talking it over."

"So that's why you're here."

"I'm lucky I got to you before Pratt did."

The Widow Stanton emerged from the house. "Supper's on, folks."

"Thank you," said Emmy.

The widow woman went back inside. Shell headed for the door.

"Shell?"

"Yeah."

"I'm glad you're here."

He smiled, relieved. "Well, I won't be much longer if I don't get some grub. Come on, Emmy. Let's eat."

The Widow Stanton took pride in her cooking, and with good reason, decided Shell, as he started on his second helping of stew and appropriated his third chunk of cornbread. As a rule he ate only enough to take the bite off his hunger, a habit developed in his younger days when he'd had to make his meager provisions last, but he'd been three days on the trail with nothing but coffee and corn dodgers to dine on, and his belt buckle was just about stuck to his backbone.

Besides, this chuck was a sight better than the victuals Lopez brewed up. Lopez was the old *vaquero* who'd been with the Rimfire outfit from the get-go. He'd been with Sam Gunnison when Sam was just getting started, brushpopping wild cattle to make the Rimfire herd. Getting along in years, Lopez was too old for brushpopping steers or busting broncs these days, so he cooked for the crew. Cowboys had several unflattering nicknames for cooks—"belly cheaters" and "grub spoilers" to name a couple—and in Shell's opinion Lopez lived up to every last one of them.

Emmy, sitting next to him at the table, also demonstrated a healthy appetite. Teague was at the foot of the table. Across from Shell, Killough was eating in a desultory manner, as though food was one of the least important things in life. Shell thought that a little odd, since Killough had made a point of complimenting the widow woman's cooking. Yet the gambler appeared to be lost in melancholy thoughts. And he was looking at Emmy quite a lot, noticed the Rimfire foreman.

Sitting beside Killough, Grissom made a pig of himself, stuffing his mouth to overflowing, dividing his attention between the food and the gambler, contemplating the latter with open animosity.

The Widow Stanton sat at the head of the table. Finishing her meal, a modest helping, she went to the kitchen and fetched an enamelware coffeepot. As she refilled Shell's cup with good Peaberry java, she glanced with mild reproof across the table at Grissom.

"I suppose I ought to be flattered, the way you attack those vittles, Mr. Grissom," she said, her tone making it clear that his atrocious table manners did not endear him to her at all.

Grissom just grunted. His mouth was full.

Killough said, "Ma'am, I've dined in the finest eateries San Francisco and New Orleans have to offer, and I can honestly say that seldom have I enjoyed finer meals than those which grace your table."

"Thank you, Mr. Killough. You're very kind. But you've scarcely touched your food this evening."

"Slick talker, ain't he?" sneered Grissom. "'Bout as slick with words as he is with them cards of his."

"Thank you, Mr. Grissom," said Killough with cool civility. "And may I say that you are as gracious a diner as you are a loser at the poker table."

Grissom's face darkened with anger. "It's awful hard to win at your table, Killough."

The Widow Stanton recognized trouble when she saw it, and was accustomed to heading it off when it appeared under her roof.

"Keep a short rein on your temper, Mr. Grissom," she advised sternly. "There'll be no donnybrook in my house. I do not relish scrubbing blood off my walls."

Shell had a hunch she had done just that in the past, which was why, no doubt, she required all those who sat at her table to leave their gun rigs in the hallway. The Rimfire foreman didn't much like being so far removed from his Remington. What if Pratt chose this moment to show up? The whole business made Shell plenty nervous. He almost wished Pratt would appear. That would be better, in a way, than not knowing where the man was or when he would make his move.

"Oh I ain't gonna hurt Mr. Killough none, ma'am," drawled Grissom. "Hey, cardsharp. You takin' the stage out in the morning?"

"I was thinking about it."

"Well, so am I. Be plenty of time to settle our differences on the road."

Making a point to ignore Grissom, Killough turned to Teague, the whiskey drummer.

"Have any luck selling your wares next door?"

"None at all," said Teague cheerfully. "The proprietor passed up a wonderful deal for the finest whiskey the world has ever tasted. Ah well."

"I thought he would. He's a purveyor of rotgut, and proud of it. The cowboys don't know any different. They'll drink anything."

"You don't have a very high opinion of cowboys, Mr. Killough," observed Shell.

"Nothing personal, I assure you. It's an honorable profession."

"Which is more than a body can say about *your* profession," said Grissom.

"I didn't force you to sit at my game."

"I thought it was an honest one."

Killough's jaws were clenched. "That's the second time you have implied that I am a cheat. Believe me, sir, I don't have to cheat to take your money. You are a poor poker player. But if you so much as halfway question my honesty again, I'll blow your brains out. I'm a good shot and I can hit a small target."

Grissom stood up so quickly that he overturned his chair. "Try me!" he shouted, spitting food. His hand dropped to his hip—and then he realized that he wasn't heeled. His head swiveled towards the door to the hallway where his guns were hanging on a row of wall pegs.

"Sit down, Mr. Grissom!" barked the Widow Stanton sharply.

Grissom glanced at her, then at the door again.

Shell stood up. "Sit down."

He spoke with a ferocious quiet which seemed to pierce the fog of rage befuddling Grissom. The youth swallowed hard and sat down. As soon as he was down Emmy was up.

"Mrs. Stanton, that was delicious. Thank you. I think I'll turn in now. It's been a long day."

"You must be exhausted, poor dear."

"Yes, ma'am. Good evening, gentlemen."

"Good evening," said Killough and Teague, almost in unison. Grissom kept his mouth shut, aware that Shell was watching him.

Shell followed Emmy out of the dining room, retrieved his Remington, and climbed the stairs behind her. At the door to her room she gave him a funny half-smile.

"If you're going to stick this close to me all night, you're going to have to marry me, Shell Harper."

Shell blushed furiously. "No, ma'am. I mean . . . well, I want to check the room, at least."

"By all means." She opened the door and gestured for him to enter. "Remember to look under the bed for the boogie man."

Shell was halfway into the room. He turned sharply.

"Look, Emmy. This is serious. If Pratt gets a hold of you he'll . . . "

"He'll what? Kill me? You said Buckhorn doesn't want me dead."

Shell grimaced. He could not bring himself to mention what lay in store for her if Buckhorn succeeded in his scheme.

"Never mind." He lighted the lamp on the bedside table and checked the room—including under the bed. Satisfied, he exited. "All clear. No boogie man. Good night, Emmy."

"Good night." No longer was she smiling. "Shell, I'm sorry. I don't mean to make light of it. It's just that . . . well, I feel very safe when I'm with you. I know you wouldn't let anything happen to me."

"I wouldn't."

She smiled and closed the door.

Shell settled down in a straight-back chair at the end of the hall. Killough came up the stairs.

"You're welcome to half of my room," offered the gambler.

"Thanks, but no."

Killough glanced at Emmy's door, and nodded. "Watchdog?"

"Something like that. Where's Grissom?"

"The saloon. Did you give him that busted lip?"

Shell nodded.

"One of us may have to shoot him before we get to Killeen," said the gambler. "Good night."

Killough entered his room. Shell leaned the chair back against the wall and prepared himself for a long vigil.

7

Shell started to doze off when the pearl-gray light of dawn began to seep through the window at the other end of the upstairs hall. When the Widow Stanton came out of her room, even though she tried to be quiet, he woke with a start and nearly pitched sideways in the rickety chair.

"Didn't mean to wake you," she said.

"Doesn't matter."

She went downstairs. Shell got up, tried to stretch the kinks out of his lanky frame. Then he went to the window and checked the street of Spanish Station. The only thing moving was a stray yellow hound meandering around the general store.

Where are you, Pratt, damn you.

Catfooting over to Emmy's door, Shell listened a moment. No sound. He got that anxious feeling again. What if she wasn't in there? How long had he been dozing? Had he checked the window in that room last night? No, he remembered now he hadn't. There was no help for it. He opened the door and peeked inside.

Emmy was sound asleep. A shapely leg, from the knee down, was outside the covers. He looked at the leg, and at the tousled chestnut hair, and he had a funny feeling in his chest. Felt fresh resolve, too.

Pratt would have to kill him to get his hands on Emmy Gunnison.

The Widow Stanton appeared at the bottom of the stairs. Shell closed the door and went down to take the cup of steaming fresh-brewed java from her with a heartfelt *gracias.*

"You two are in some kind of trouble," she said, and it wasn't a question.

He nodded, but did not offer to elaborate.

"Has something to do with that man you asked about when you first showed up here, doesn't it?"

"Yes, ma'am."

"He means to do your lady friend harm?"

Shell flashed a weary smile. "You're right on the money, Mrs. Stanton."

"I pegged you for some kind of trouble when I first laid eyes on you. But you're not so bad. Must be getting old and senile. Used to be a good judge of men. You're just *in* trouble."

"Yeah." Shell sighed. "About my horse. Could you figure out a way to get her to Killeen, at least?"

"Where you headed?"

"Lampasas."

"I'll just have him tied onto the back of the next southbound. Be one week."

"That'll do fine. Thanks."

She nodded. "I'd best go get breakfast started."

Shell trudged back upstairs. He was almost finished with his coffee when Emmy emerged from her room, wearing a yellow wrapper. She stared at Shell.

"Did you sit up all night?"

He just shrugged. "I wasn't all that tired."

She looked at him for a long time in a tousled, sleepy way that gave him that funny feeling all over again, only stronger this time. At length she held out her hand.

"Give me that charcoal-burner of yours, Shell."

"What for?"

"Do you work for me now?"

"I reckon so."

"Then do what I say."

He handed her the Remington. She tested the weight of the six-shooter, then rolled it like a gun artist.

"Okay. Now you don't have to shadow me twenty-four hours a day."

"I don't really mind."

She smiled, a quirky half-smile that had a lot of meaning hidden behind it, none of which he would ever figure out, not in a million years.

"Used to," she said, "you didn't like to be tied down too tight to anything."

He looked at the tips of his down-at-heel boots. "That was in my younger days, when I didn't know any better."

"Maybe you *have* changed. But I can still outshoot you, Shell Harper. So don't fret about me. I promise I'll kill the first stranger I see."

"I think I'll just take a look around outside before breakfast."

"You do that," she said, and went back into the room and closed the door.

He stood there a moment, then rapped his knuckles on the door.

She opened it. "Yes?"

"I recollect a key in that lock, Emmy."

"Oh. Okay."

"You didn't lock it last night."

"I didn't need to. You were here."

She shut the door, and turned the key.

Shell drew the Winchester rifle from the boot strapped to his saddle and went downstairs. Leaving the empty coffee cup on the sideboard in the hall, he stepped out onto the porch. The sky was lighting up fast. It was cool enough now, but Shell calculated that the day would wind up plenty hot before it was done. Across the street stood the stagecoach. The yellow dog was sniffing the wheels, picking up strange scents from far-off places. From the livery came the clang and clatter of a smitty's hammer on iron. *Probably Jesus*, thought Shell. *Has the forge going already*.

The Rimfire foreman shoulder-racked the Winchester and angled across the street towards Cosper's store. The door was open. Billy Bishop was handcuffed to a hitching post in front of the she-bang. He was squatting like a bronco Apache under the rail. His furtive coyote eyes watched Shell cross the hard-pack. Shell knew nothing about the man, but instinct and experience told him enough. You didn't have to be well-acquainted with rattlesnakes to know better than to get too close to one.

He wondered where the Texas Ranger was.

As Shell passed Bishop to step up onto the she-bang's boardwalk the outlaw spoke.

"Hey, cowboy. Got the makings?"

"No."

Shell turned away from Bishop, only to find the doorway blocked by Jack Ember. The Henry repeater was cradled in the craggy Ranger's arms.

"You got business with my prisoner, friend?" There was a hard challenge in his flat, unemotional delivery.

"No more than I have with you."

Ember blinked. He wasn't accustomed to folks talking up to him. The ghost of a smile flickered beneath his bushy mustache.

"That's Billy Bishop. He's murderin' scum. My name's Ember. C Company, Texas Rangers. My job's to get Bishop to Austin. Now, why don't you be a gentleman and introduce yourself?"

"Shell Harper."

"A cowboy?"

"The Rimfire, down Lampasas way."

Eyes narrowing, Ember cocked his head slightly. "Ain't that Sam Gunnison's spread?"

"Used to be. He's dead."

"Sorry to hear that. He was a helluva man."

"Yes, he was."

"You thinking about riding that stage out of here?"

"Planned on it. Also thought I might give Mr. Cosper some of my business."

Ember stepped aside and let him pass.

Ike Cosper stood behind the dry-goods counter, a potbellied man, baldheaded and rough-hewn. His place was stocked to the rafters with all manner of goods, for when it came to supplying the handful of hardscrabble spreads in the vicinity of Spanish Stations he had the market cornered. Blankets, clothes, "airtights," hats and boots, rope and tackle, lanterns, work implements, firearms and ammunition, a few bolts of fabric and bonnets for the ladies—the inventory was virtually endless.

"Cartridges," said Shell. "A box of .44s."

When Cosper returned with the box of "beans" Shell said, "Seen a stranger hereabouts the last couple of days? Black beard, gray duster, rides a gray horse."

Cosper shook his head. As Shell paid for the cartridges Ember came up to the counter.

"Expecting trouble, Harper?"

"I like to be ready, just in case."

"Think something bad's gonna happen it usually does," chimed in Cosper, a crackerbox philosopher if ever there was one.

"No need to worry," said Ember. "Won't be no trouble coming your way."

"How do you figure?"

"What the Ranger means," said Cosper, "is that he aims to commandeer the southbound stage."

"There'll be another one along in a week or so," said Ember.

"By my count there's five people planning to ride that stage this morning, including me."

"That's five people who get a whole week to enjoy the pleasures of Spanish Station. And the widow woman's cooking."

Shell said, "I can't speak for the others, but I'm not inclined to wait another week."

"You might could buy a horse from one of the ranches nearby."

"Might? I haven't got the money to spend on a bottomed-out hayburner. Besides, I'd need two."

"Two? How come?"

"I'm traveling with a lady."

"Take the next stage," said Ember gruffly.

"Sounds like you're the one expecting trouble."

"I won't do-si-do with you, cowboy. I figure there's a good chance that Billy's boys will have a go at setting him loose before we get to Austin. Now, the last thing I need when that happens is a bunch of civilians getting in the line of fire. So take the next stage. That ain't a request."

8

Shell thought it over. Would Emmy be safer here at Spanish Station or on the stage to Killeen? Looked like six of one and half dozen of another. But there was also a chance that the Bishop Gang wouldn't make an appearance. And Pratt probably wouldn't try to take Emmy off a stage full of people—including a Texas Ranger. The fact remained that the only safe place for Emmy was the Rimfire, and the sooner they got there the better.

"Maybe you could use some help," said Shell.

"Why would you want to do that?"

"I reckon Billy Bishop and his gallop-and-gunshot boys have been giving the folks of this state a hard time for quite a spell. It's in everybody's best interests to see Bishop behind bars."

"Behind bars, hell." Ember snorted. "The boy'll stretch hemp, and he and his hardcase hands know it. They'll kill anybody that gets in the way of saving him from the hangman's noose, and won't think twice about it."

"Sounds like they're mighty loyal to Bishop."

"Loyalty's got nothing in the world to do with it. We don't know the identity of everybody who rides with Billy. But we will. He'll sing like a little canary when he sees that rope with his name on it. Tell us who they are and where we can find them. I'd bet my badge on that. And they know it, too. They've got to save Billy's bacon, or he'll drag them all down to hell with him if he can."

"If I go along it'll be that much harder for them."

"You have a pretty high opinion of yourself, cowboy."

Shell smiled. "I'd say you were the one. You aim to take on the whole Bishop Gang single-handed."

"Buck Stonecipher and A. T. Rand are meeting me in Killeen. I'd match those two Rangers against the entire owlhoot population of the Bloody Border."

"Maybe so, but it's a long way to Killeen."

Ember was regarding Shell in a more favorable light now. "You've got sand, that's certain." He thought it over, then nodded curtly. "Okay, Harper. You want to get yourself killed, that's your lookout."

"And the others?"

"Talk 'em out of it. Convince them to stay put. That way they'll stay healthy."

"At least one will have to come with me."

"Your lady friend?" Ember shook his head. "I've always been of the opinion that women are trouble. And a woman on this ride damn sure would be."

"It's Emmy Gunnison. She can shoot better than any man I know, and isn't bashful about pulling the trigger, either."

"Big Sam's daughter?"

"The one and only."

"Then I reckon she can shoot. Okay, cowboy. You've got yourself a deal. I hope you don't live to regret it. If you get yourself killed don't come crying to me about it. 'Cause I tried to warn you."

Everybody who had been present at dinner the night before was at the table again for breakfast, with the addition of O'Hara, the stagecoach driver, who ate like three men and uttered effusive compliments to the

Widow Stanton between every helping. Mr. Teague, the whiskey drummer, was as ebullient as always. The gambler, Killough, again barely touched his food. As for Grissom, the young would-be gunslinger looked green around the gills. Shell figured he was hung over from an all-night drinking binge.

The Rimfire foreman consumed a respectable stack of flapjacks swimming in molasses and thick rashers of crisp bacon before informing the others of Ranger Jack Ember's plan to appropriate the stagecoach.

A moment of stunned silence followed Shell's laconic delivery of the facts as he knew them. Then Teague looked at O'Hara and said, "He can't do that. I've got a living to make. Can't make it in this one-horse town. No offense, ma'am. He can't do that . . . can he, Mr. O'Hara?"

O'Hara had resumed eating. Nothing—neither earthquakes nor Indian raids nor Texas Rangers—could interfere with his appetite.

"He's a Ranger," replied the reinsman. "He can do whatever the heck he wants to do."

"That's what he aimed to do at first," said Shell. "I persuaded him to let Emmy and me go along. Thing is, the Ranger figures Billy Bishop's saddle partners are going to take a stab at cutting him loose."

"You must not think that's too likely," observed Killough. "Else you wouldn't put the lady in jeopardy."

"She's a better shot with a rifle and sidegun than I am," said Shell. He glanced at Emmy. "Of course, if you'd rather not take the chance . . . "

"I want to get home. I've been delayed long enough."

"That's what I thought you'd say. But Ember advises the rest of you to stay put and wait for the next stage. So do I. Emmy and I have to go. But if you don't have to, don't."

"'The Worldly Hope men set their Hearts upon Turns Ashes—or its prospers; and anon, like Snow upon the Desert's dusty Face, Lighting a little Hour or two—is gone.'"

Shell stared blankly across the table at the gambler. "What does that mean, whittled down?"

"*The Rubáiyát*," said Emmy. "Omar Khayyám."

"Why, yes," said Killough, pleasantly surprised. "I make my living bucking the odds. I wouldn't be much of a gambling man if I didn't. And besides, my life is not so valuable that I mind risking it."

"I reckon you must be heeled," said Shell.

"Indeed." Killough reached under his coat and brandished a pearl-handled, over-and-under derringer.

Grissom snorted at sight of the hideout. "That peashooter wouldn't stop a full-growed jackrabbit."

"You'd be surprised," said the gambler, and put the gun away.

"What about you, Mr. Teague?" asked Shell.

"Why no, I-I don't carry a firearm," stammered the whiskey drummer. "In fact, I must confess I have never fired one in anger."

"You'd best stay here and wait for the next stage."

"No, no. I'll go along. I must move on. I . . . if I don't make some sales pretty soon I'll be out of a job."

Shell turned to Grissom. "You?"

"I ain't never backed down from no kind of trouble."

"Miss Gunnison, I urge you to reconsider," said the Widow Stanton. "Stay here. Just one week. What might happen . . . " She shook her head. "It would be no place for a lady."

"I don't know that I'm a lady," said Emmy, "but I was born a Texan. I'll take my chances."

O'Hara put down his knife and fork, wiped his mouth with a napkin, and consulted the Regulator on the wall.

"Mighty fine vittles, Mrs. Stanton, thank you."

He rose from the table and headed for the hallway, rubbing his belly. "Stage rolls in twenty minutes. All's goin' better come on."

When he saw Emmy carrying her two valises down the stairs Killough put down his one small carpetbag and came to the rescue. "I'd be honored if you'd allow me, ma'am."

"That's not necessary, really. Thank you all the same."

"I'd deem it an honor."

Emmy surrendered before such gallantry, and gave him the valises. Killough threw Shell a wry glance. The Rimfire foreman was descending the stairs behind Emmy, burdened with his own saddle and war bag.

"Don't worry, cowboy. I'm not horning in on your range," said the gambler with an infuriating chuckle.

Emmy tried to repress a smile. Shell tried not to look as embarrassed as he felt.

In the hall, the Widow Stanton gave Emmy a hug.

"You men make certain no harm comes to this child," she admonished Shell and Killough.

"Yes, ma'am," said Shell.

"You can rely on me," assured the gambler, with a short bow.

Shell ignored him, or tried to. The gambler was having his fun, and trying to get Shell's goat.

They left the house and crossed the street to the stagecoach. Jesus had the team ready in the traces. O'Hara was making his walk-around, checking the harness and the wheels and undercarriage, using a clasp knife to carve a chew off a plug of Union Leader as he worked. Shell didn't see Teague or Grissom. But he did see the Texas Ranger, escorting his prisoner over from Cosper's general store. Billy Bishop's coyote eyes sparkled as his gaze roamed all over Emmy.

"Whowee!" he cried. "Lookit what I'm gonna get. And it ain't even my birthday!"

Ember planted a boot in Bishop's backside, propelling the hardcase face first into the dust. Shackled, Bishop could scarcely break his fall. He rolled over on his back and lay there, glowering at the Ranger in a hot and murderous rage.

"Keep your trap shut and your eyes to yourself," advised Ember.

"I'm gonna enjoy watching you die, Ranger."

"Better hurry. Your days are numbered. I calculate you'll be hanging from a rope in a fortnight."

O'Hara put Emmy's valises and Killough's carpetbag in the rear boot. Then he clambered up into the box and motioned for Shell to hand him the saddle and war bag. These items were deposited on the top rack. Ember eyed the gambler.

"Tired of living?" asked the Ranger.

"I am sometimes."

Teague and Grissom were crossing the street from the widow's house, the whiskey drummer struggling with his big case.

"That'll have to go up top," said O'Hara. The reinsman glanced at Grissom. "Where's your gear?"

"All I got's the shirt on my back . . . and this." Grissom patted the Starr Colt in its holster.

"Then you are mighty poor," opined O'Hara.

"One more hand of poker," joked Killough, "and he'd have lost the shirt."

"Shut up, cardsharp," said Grissom

Ember turned to Shell. "You did a bang-up job of talking everybody out of coming along, cowboy."

Shell shrugged. "It's a free country."

The Ranger just grunted.

"If the circus is over, you all can get aboard now," said O'Hara, having manhandled Teague's heavy case up onto the top rack. "By my count, we've got one too many to ride inside."

Ember hauled Billy Bishop to his feet and shoved him towards the door of the coach. Teague and Grissom demonstrated that they had every intention of riding in the coach, too.

"Looks like it's you or me," Killough told Shell.

Shell didn't cotton to the idea of riding up top while Emmy was stuck inside with the likes of Grissom and Billy Bishop. So he was all set to make a case of it when Emmy spoke up.

"You ride topside, Shell," she said.

"But Emmy . . ."

"I'll be fine. Mr. Killough will keep Grissom in line. Won't you, Mr. Killough?"

"Rest assured, ma'am. If he doesn't act the perfect gentleman, I will throw him out of the coach."

"If there's trouble," Emmy told Shell, "I'd rather you and your rifle were up there with Mr. O'Hara."

"You're the boss," muttered Shell.

"Permit me," said Killough, and helped Emmy into the coach. He flashed a wry smile at Shell as he climbed in after her.

Disgruntled, Shell hauled himself up into the box and settled next to O'Hara, reaching back for his saddle and the Winchester in its scabbard.

"There's a scattergun under the seat, if you prefer," said the reinsman, threading the ribbons between his strong callused fingers.

"I'll keep that in mind," said Shell, but extracted the repeater from its scabbard just the same.

"We'll be fine," said O'Hara. "I've done for my share of road agents in my time, believe you me. Have I got some stories to tell. If Billy Bishop's wild bunch shows up we'll make short work of them."

Shell didn't say anything. Discounting Teague and Grissom, there were five on the coach who could make smoke and probably hit what they were aiming at if came down to lead-slinging. That included Emmy. So maybe the jehu's confidence was justified. Maybe. Nonetheless, Shell couldn't muster up much confidence. It wasn't so much Bishop's boys as it was Pratt. *Where the blazes was Buckhorn's hired gun?*

O'Hara released the brake and slapped the leathers, hollering bloody murder at the leaders. It was a smooth break, and as they rolled down Spanish Station's abbreviated street Shell glanced over his shoulder and saw the Widow Stanton standing in the shade of her porch.

Weighed down with a keen sense of impending doom, the widow woman watched the stage until a bend in the road took it out of sight. She had a nose for trouble . . .

9

Addicks Bell and Joaquin Cruz held their cow ponies
to a walk as they crossed a meadow hemmed in by
brush-covered Rimfire hills. A jackrabbit whipped
through the tan grass in front of them. On the slope to
the right of them came a sudden explosion of wings as
a covey of quail burst into the hot, blue sky. Addicks
jumped in his saddle. His hand fell to the sidegun on
his hip. Not that he could have hit anything had he
drawn and fired. But he sure could have thrown some
lead around.

When he saw that quail were the culprits, he grimaced and glanced, embarrassed, at Joaquin. The
vaquero was trying to suppress a grin, with only
mediocre success.

"What's so funny?"

"*Nada.*"

Addicks snickered. "Sure, I'm a little jumpy.
Anybody with a lick of sense would be."

"A little? You are as jumpy as bacon on a hot skil-
let, *amigo.*"

"There are rumored to be rustlers in these parts,
remember?"

"I remember. But rustlers don't have wings."

Addicks yanked the brim of his sweat-stained hat

low over his eyes. "We've been riding since can-see, Joaquin. Don't you think it's time we loosened a cinch?"

Joaquin consulted the blazing sun and its position in the sky, and concurred. They dismounted at the edge of the meadow, collected some deadwood from a nearby clump of scrub cedar, and built a small fire. Addicks broke out the coffeepot, poured some water from his canteen into it, and measured out a few handfuls of Sultano coffee from a pouch he carried among his possibles. While the coffee boiled and their ponies grazed, Joaquin spread his blanket and stretched his lean frame on the ground. Sombrero balanced on his face, he prepared for a short *siesta*. Addicks had extracted a book of poetry from his saddlebags. He tried to read a Shakespearean sonnet, but his thoughts kept straying to Shell Harper.

"You think Shell's okay?" he asked the *vaquero*.

"*Sí.*"

A little while later, Addicks said, "I wonder if Emmy Gunnison will hold onto the Rimfire. You think she will? I sure don't cotton to working for the likes of Moss Buckhorn."

Joaquin just grunted.

A few minutes later Addicks gave up on Shakespeare and said, "I don't much care for the idea of riding the grub line, or even riding for another brand."

With a sigh, Joaquin sat up and pushed back the sombrero.

"Did you hear something?" asked Addicks, alarmed.

"Yes. You, *amigo.*"

"Sorry about that. Want some coffee?"

Addicks used his bandanna to protect his hand while he poured java from the pot into two tin cups. But as he handed one cup to Joaquin the *vaquero* leaped to his feet, so suddenly that Addicks spilled hot coffee on his hand anyway.

"What is it?" asked Addicks.

"Listen!"

Addicks listened. At first he heard nothing. Was Joaquin pulling his leg? Was he setting up some kind of practical joke? That was one of the *vaquero*'s favorite pastimes.

The Illinois plowboy-turned-cowboy had been the brunt of so many practical jokes in his time that he was almost paranoid about it.

Then he heard it. Cattle. They were worked up over something.

"It's coming from yonder, about a mile, maybe less," he said.

Joaquin nodded. He swept up his blanket and turned to his horse. Addicks kicked dirt over the fire. He didn't have time to retrieve the coffeepot because Joaquin was already on the move. Hastily climbing into his saddle, Addicks thought, *Ain't that always the way?* Now he was going to have to traipse all the way back here to recover that coffeepot just because Joaquin didn't have the decency to wait for him to collect his gear. The *vaquero* was an easy-going, devil-may-care character most of the time—a man who made it a point never to hurry, unless it was a truly important matter. Obviously he thought those cattle were important, because he was hurrying now, moving like greased lightning, already mounted and riding into the brush before Addicks could even fork his horse.

Before long they found themselves hidden in a thicket of scrub oak, on the rim of a hogback ridge, peering down through the tangle at the clearing below.

There were four men in the clearing. One was tending a small fire. Near him stood a second, wearing thick gloves, and poking a branding iron into the blaze. The other two were mounted. While one of them held some fifteen cattle pinned against a crescent-shaped cutbank, the other was dragging a stubborn steer over to the fire, one end of his lasso around the longhorn's neck, the other lashed to the biscuit of his saddle.

"Rustlers, sure enough," muttered Addicks. "Recognize any of them?"

Joaquin shook his head.

"Me neither. If we ride to the house and bring back the outfit it'll be slap dark before we can get back here."

Joaquin nodded.

"Those cross-branders would probably be long gone by then."

Joaquin didn't nod his head, or shake it, or say anything this time. He sat there, leaning forward in the saddle, watching the four rustlers with the unblinking intensity of a hawk peering at its prey.

"So what are we going to do?" asked Addicks.

"What we are paid to do, *amigo*."

"We're outnumbered. Or doesn't that matter to you?"

"Not to me." The *vaquero* flashed a grin, but he still didn't take his eyes off the rustlers.

Addicks sighed. He removed his see-betters and rubbed the dust off the lenses with a corner of his bandanna. "I'm not a real good shot, you'll remember."

"I know. I was thinking we could ride in on them from opposite directions and catch them in a crossfire. But then you might accidentally shoot me."

Addicks felt inadequate to the task at hand, and even though Joaquin was joking—or at least half-joking— the comment did little to bolster his needy confidence.

Down below, the firetender had shaken out his lariat and lassoed the steer's hind legs, stretching him out. The man with the iron moved in and burned a mark on the muley-back's flank. The steer bawled helplessly as the red-hot iron scorched its hide. The distance was too great for Joaquin to make out the brand on the cowponies, or to tell what mark was being put on the Rimfire cattle. As for Addicks, he couldn't have made out an elephant, had there been one standing down there in the clearing, with his glasses off.

"So we will ride in together," said Joaquin. He drew his repeater from its saddle boot. Addicks donned his spectacles, pulled his Colt revolver from its holster, flipped open the gate and turned the cylinder to the empty chamber he kept under the hammer as a precaution, filling it with a bullet plucked from a loop in his gunbelt.

"Ready?" asked Joaquin.

Addicks envied the *vaquero* his unflappable calm. "Ready as I'll ever be," he replied.

They led their horses down the slope single-file, Joaquin in the lead, making as little noise as humanly possible passing through the brush. Reaching the base of the slope undetected, they climbed back into the saddles. Out in the clearing, the mounted rope artist had tossed a loop over the horns of another steer in the small herd and proceeded to drag it, with the invaluable assistance of his well-trained cow pony, closer to the fire.

Addicks and Joaquin rode out into the open.

"That's all!" shouted Addicks. "Nobody move!"

He aimed his short-gun in the general direction of the nearest men, the firetender and the one with the iron. Joaquin had rifle to shoulder and was covering the mounted rope artist.

The four rustlers froze, caught completely by surprise.

"Let those *pistolas* hit the ground, pronto," ordered Joaquin.

The two men who were afoot seemed inclined to obey. Their horses were tethered to a greasewood a good thirty feet away, a greater distance than that which separated them from the two Rimfire riders. The man in Joaquin's rifle sights wasn't eager to make a fatal mistake, either, especially with his hands full of "hard twist" lariat. But the rider keeping the cows bunched operated under no such constraints. He took one look at the situation and made his play. Drawing his revolver, he fired at the Rimfire men.

The shot went wide. Joaquin swung his rifle and returned fire. The bullet sang off the stone lip of the cutbank. The rustler didn't bother trying for a second shot. He spurred his horse into a gallop, heading for the tall timber. Spooked by the gun talk, the cattle scattered, bawling. Joaquin jacked another round into the repeater's chamber and fired again, then again, determined to drop the man who had shot at him.

The third time was the charm. The bullet knocked the rustler sideways out of his saddle, into the path of a dozen hard-running cattle.

The other rustlers were slapping leather. "Every man for himself!" bellowed the firetender, running for his horse and slinging lead at Addicks and Joaquin. A bullet plucked the sleeve of Joaquin's shirt. Realizing what an inviting target he made in the saddle, the *vaquero* dismounted. Addicks took a shot at the fire-tender from the back of his pivoting horse, and missed by a country mile. Meanwhile, the rope artist was plunging into the brush, low in the saddle. The man with the branding iron was standing his ground, blasting away. Joaquin plugged him in the chest. The man tottered backwards on his heels, fired his last round at the sky, and toppled over into the dust.

That left two. The firetender forked his horse and lit out, hell for leather. The rope artist had already vanished into the *brasada*. Addicks dug spur and went after the former. "I'll take this one," he yelled at Joaquin.

He chased the rustler for almost a mile, across the rough country, thick with scrub that clutched at his shirt and chaps and tore at his face. But Addicks stuck to it. He didn't gain ground but he didn't lose much either.

Crashing through some cedar, he found himself in

a meadow bisected by a wagon trace. The rustler was nearly across the meadow, but right before he reached the thicket on the other side he suddenly checked his horse and spun it around and fired a shot at Addicks. The Rimfire hand thought he could actually hear the bullet sizzle past his ear. Shaken, he reined his horse in and fired back. To his amazement, he hit the mark. It was all the rustler could do to stay in the saddle. Addicks' slug had mangled his left shoulder. He turned his horse sharply and kicked it into motion. The horse charged up a slope heavy with scrub. Addicks went after him with a vengeance.

Reaching the crest of a hill, Addicks checked his horse. He could see where the rustler's pony had gone slipping and sliding down the steep slope, and he could see the horse itself, riderless now, down in a rock-strewn gulch. But where was the rustler? Had he fallen from the saddle during the descent? There was no sign of him. Addicks felt his skin crawl. He didn't like this, not one bit.

The pony down below suddenly sprouted a third pair of legs. Addicks heard the slap, saw the horse gallop away, revealing the rustler—and he realized he'd been fooled by an old Indian trick. The rustler had been hanging on the other side of the horse, hidden from Addicks' view. As the man raised his gun, Addicks fired at him—and missed.

The rustler didn't miss.

A giant invisible fist punched Addicks in the chest, stunning him so that he did not even feel the fall as he pitched from the saddle. He was next aware of lying flat on his back, the sun in his eyes, and rocks jabbing him in the spine. He tried to move, but couldn't. That scared him. His whole body was numb, cold. Worse still, he couldn't seem to get enough air. It felt like his lungs had collapsed. The blue Texas sky suddenly turned dark, and he drifted away.

10

The tortured creaking of the weatherbeaten old buck-board intruded on the twilight hush. The two mules in the worn and oft-mended traces had seen better days. They plodded along without enthusiasm, conveying the buckboard along the trace which angled across a meadow hemmed in by the *brasada* hills.

The driver of the wagon was a young woman. Her name was Mattie, and she was not yet twenty. Her slender frame was clad in plain, brown gingham, a dress faded and mended in places and not a little too large for the willowy girl who wore it. Mattie's hair was long and dark-brown and woven into a French braid. Her feet were bare. She had a pair of shoes, but she seldom wore them, not knowing when she might possess another, and not wanting to wear them out.

Though a smudge of dirt adorned her chin and cheek, she was pretty. Bright, alert brown eyes took in every aspect of the world around her, and appreciated all of it. She liked this time of day best of all, when the shades of dusk softened the harsh lines of the hill country, and the setting sun painted the bottoms of purple mare's tail clouds pink and orange. But she did not like the nighttime. Her mother had died in the night, and it seemed as though all the really bad things that had ever happened to her had happened in the night.

She saw the horse, grazing in the cedars at the base of the hill west of the wagon trace, and it raised its head to look at her, and whicker softly. Making note of the empty saddle, Mattie wondered where the rider could be. Maybe the horse had gotten away from its owner, and left him afoot. What should she do? She knew what her pa would do in her place. He'd tie the horse to the back of the wagon and take it home, and if no one came along to claim it, well, they would own a horse. "Possession is nine-tenths of the law." That was one of Liam Henshaw's favorite sayings. He had a knack for finding things that other people had lost, so it was only natural that he thought that way.

Mattie hauled up on the leathers to stop the mules. Knobheads were hard to get started, but just as hard to stop. They just seemed to make being stubborn an art in itself. Still uncertain of what to do, Mattie wrapped the leathers around the brake pole and climbed down out of the wagon. She pulled up a handful of grass and approached the horse, holding the grass out, an offering of friendship, and the horse watched her. If it could have comprehended the gentle innocence in her face it would not have hesitated to approach her. But it did hesitate, because the events of only a few hours ago had made it skittish. So did the smell of blood.

Moving slowly, Mattie got close enough for the horse to stretch its neck and sniff the grass, nibble at it, then snicker and paw the ground and take a step forward. Mattie wasn't intimidated. She stood still, and smiled, and the horse pulled the grass out of her hand, eyed her as it ate, and then nudged her shoulder. She stroked its blazed muzzle. Then she saw the blood smear on the saddle.

Someone had been hurt. Maybe killed. The sight of blood did not frighten her. Only the night frightened her.

Knowing a little something about reading signs, she could tell that a horse, presumably this one, had gone up the wooded slope and then come back down. So she started up the hill. The rocky ground did not even slow her down. The soles of her small feet were tough. From the crest of the rise she looked down the other side, down into the gulch, and she saw Addicks, sprawled on the far slope, thirty feet below the rim. She gasped, a hand flying to her mouth. Was he dead? He looked dead. A big splotch of blood had dried on his shirt, almost black now, and flies were buzzing around it.

Mattie went to him, knelt at his side. She thought his chest was moving, but she wasn't sure. If it was moving it sure wasn't much. Leaning over, she put her ear close to his mouth, hoping to hear the breath in his throat. The braided hair slipped over her shoulder and brushed his cheek. His head moved then, and a low moan escaped his lips. Startled, Mattie jerked away.

He had been shot, high in the chest. She saw the bullethole in his shirt. She'd seen gunshot men before. Her father's eternal wanderings had taken them to some pretty rough places, and Mattie had witnessed her share of frontier violence.

Addicks was slowly swimming to the surface of a pool of cold, black oblivion. His eyelids flickered. He could discern a blurred shape in the dusky gloom, and knew that someone was there. But who? What had happened? Yes, that was it—he'd been shot. Was he still alive? Then the pain struck him. It felt as though his chest had been crushed, his rib cage smashed into a thousand sharp bone slivers. Panic gripped him, and he clutched at the shape looming over him. He did not want to die alone. He did not want to die period, but if he had to, not alone.

Mattie did not recoil when he clutched her arm, although the hand was caked with blood. The man was trying to say something. His lips were moving, but the weak sounds coming forth bore no resemblance to words. She wondered how long he had been lying here. A spell, by the looks of it. Maybe he wanted some water. Yes, that must be what he was trying to say. She tried to pull her arm free, gently, but he was holding on, holding on for dear life, and her heart went out to him. She wished she could say something to comfort him. But she couldn't. A moment later he lapsed into unconsciousness. The hand loosened its vise-like grip on her arm.

Somewhere in the near distance a coyote yapped. A flurry of leathery wings drew her attention skyward. Bats, flitting overhead, were quick jerky shapes against a blue velvet sky already sprinkled with the first stars. There were many limestone caves in these hills, and many bats lived in those caves. She didn't like bats, or the lonesome sound of the coyote, and wished she were home, because her father liked to scare her with stories about wild Comanches, and he said they still roamed this country, and would do unspeakable things to her if they caught her.

But she couldn't leave this man to die.

He was too heavy for her to get to the wagon, and she couldn't get the wagon over this hill. What could she do? Standing, she looked around at the night fast closing in—and made up her mind.

Going back down the hill, she found the horse not far from where she had fed it the grass. Tying the reins to the trunk of a scrub oak, she walked on out to the wagon, unhitched the mules, and gave them both a swat on the rump. They trotted off. Mattie was pretty sure they would go home. Mules were slow and stubborn, but that didn't mean they were stupid. Animals always seemed to know the way home.

Retrieving the horse, she led it up the hill to where the man lay. Thought about building a fire— maybe the man had some sulfur matches in his saddle- bags—but then she remembered the Comanches

again, and decided against a fire. Loosening the saddle
cinch, she untied the soogans and covered the man
with his blankets. A canteen dangled from a strap dallied around the saddlehorn, and she took that. Took
the rifle from the scabbard, too. Mattie knew about
rifles. She hunted rabbits and sage hens and such with
her father's old Spencer carbine. Someone had to do
the hunting. Her father didn't want to. And usually he
was too drunk to try. She didn't want him to try when
he was drunk. He could kill himself, accidental-like. A
lot of folks would say that would be no great loss, but
Liam Henshaw was all she had, for better or worse.

Leaving the horse tied to a tree, she sat down
next to the wounded man, sitting cross-legged, with
the rifle in her lap, and the canteen close at hand in
case he woke up again and wanted a drink. Then she
took his bloody hand in hers and held it tight. It felt
good to hold someone's hand, even the hand of a man
who quite possibly might be dead in the morning,
because the night was going to be long and dark, and
there was no telling when her father would find them.
Likely not until morning. But he would come eventually, of that Mattie was certain. For her, and for the
whiskey in the wagon. Oh, yes, he would come, with
the whiskey in the wagon and none at home.

He did come, finally, late the next morning.
Having stayed awake all night, Mattie was dozing off
as soon as the sun rose to chase away the night shadows, and by midmorning she was fast asleep, curled up
beside Addicks, holding his hand and gripping the
rifle—but not so tightly anymore.

She woke with a start, at first unsure what had
awakened her, and remembering remnants of a dream,
fast fading away, of her mother calling her in to dinner.
She was just a child, playing in the snow in front of a
nice, solid, comfortable, permanent-looking house.
Even her father looked solid and permanent, in a pros-
perous way, and that was a puzzlement, because that

wasn't at all like her father. In the dream she could clearly hear her mother's voice—a sweet, strong, kind, loving voice—but, oddly, she could never get a clear view of her mother's face.

Then she heard her father's hoarse voice. He was calling her name from down in the meadow, and the final shreds of the nice dream disintegrated. Mattie was sorry to see it go. She sat up and glanced at the gunshot man beside her. Was he still alive? Yes, breathing, but just barely. He was fighting to hold onto life, but would not live much longer without care.

Mattie pointed the rifle at the brazen sky and fired a shot. Counted to fifty, and fired again. She was almost to fifty again when her father came lumbering through the scrub like a crippled old bear.

Liam was a paunchy, balding man clad in red-faded-to-pink under-riggings tucked into stroud trousers with a hole in one knee, the trousers held in place on the downslope of his belly by a pair of suspenders. He was carrying the Spencer carbine. His face, covered with a three-day stubble, was beet-red—the climb had durn near finished him, and he was huffing like a locomotive pulling a long freight up a steep grade.

Mattie was on her feet now, and rushed to hug him.

"Now, now, gal. Are you okay?"

She nodded.

Liam stared at Addicks Bell.

"What happened here? Is he dead? Did you shoot him? Dammit, Mattie, you skeered the daylights out of me when you didn't come home last night. Lord, gal, how many times I told you not to be caught out here in the brush after sundown? Damned Comanch' coulda got their hands on you. Haven't I told you enough times what-all them red savages would do to you if they caught you? Jesus, Mattie! You're all I got that's worth anything, gal. Don't you know that? I wouldn't know what to do if I lost you. And I figured I had, sure as the turnin' of the earth. I was in a frightful state all night, Mattie, and I didn't even have no whiskey to soothe my frazzled nerves."

He disentangled himself from Mattie's embrace and ventured warily closer to Addicks. "Is he dead?" He nudged Addicks with the toe of his boot—and a second later was hopping frantically on one leg, howling like a stuck pig, and clutching his shin with both hands, having dropped the shotgun.

"Jesus, Mattie! How come you hauled off and kicked your ol' pa? I was just tryin' to see if there was a spark of life left in him."

Mattie pointed at Addicks, then raised both arms up from her sides, palms turned to the sky, and finally pointed in the direction of home.

"Take him home?"

Mattie nodded.

Liam looked at Addicks again, making note of the man's boots. A right fine pair of boots, with some good spurs strapped on, *and durned if they don't look to be just about my size.* Liam glanced at the horse yonder. Fine-looking animal, that horse, with a good-looking rig strapped to its back. And the Winchester rifle, now there was a fine firearm. Finally he checked the holster on Addicks' hip, and was disappointed to find it empty. He started scanning the ground for the missing pistol, only to realize that Mattie was watching him, and her expression warned him that she knew exactly what was going through his mind.

He smiled, sheepishly. "Mattie, gal, he's the deadest *live* man I've ever seen. If we try to move him he'll die, like as not."

She repeated the sequence of gestures to indicate that they were going to carry Addicks home, and punctuated the pantomime with a stamp of her bare foot.

Liam sighed. "But Mattie . . . "

She stamped her foot again, harder this time.

Liam was looking covetously at the horse again, but when he saw the brand the color drained out of his face.

"Jesus, Mattie! He rides for the Rimfire. We cain't take him home. We just cain't . . . "

But a look at Mattie's face informed him that this was precisely what they were going to do, and Liam Henshaw resigned himself to the inevitable.

11

That same morning, Joaquin Cruz returned to the clearing where he and Addicks had traded lead with the rustlers—one of whom was now his prisoner. The man's hands were tied behind his back, and Joaquin was leading his horse. The *vaquero* had taken the added precaution of tying the rustler's ankles together with a hobble passed under the pony's belly. This was to keep his prisoner from kicking the horse into a sudden run that just might jerk the reins out of Joaquin's grasp.

The rustler's face was a mess, bruised and swollen. One eye was almost completely shut. Joaquin had pursued him for miles before deciding to fall back and follow his sign, hoping by this ruse to lure the rustler into believing that he had given up the pursuit. It worked. The rustler not only slowed down but stopped for the night. Joaquin found his camp and slipped in on him. Wanting to take the man alive, the *vaquero* had resorted to his fists. Now he was back where the shivaree had started, looking for Addicks Bell.

The fire was cold, the cattle scattered, the branding iron lay in the dust. Joaquin retrieved that, tied it onto his saddle. He secured the rustler's reins to the gnarled root of a log and walked over to the first man he had shot, the one the cattle had trampled. The *vaquero* steeled himself and hunkered down to rifle the dead man's pockets. He found some hard money, two shiny gold double eagles. That was all. Joaquin checked the second dead man, the brand artist. Nothing. The *vaquero* glanced skyward. Turkey vultures rode the air currents, while some were perched on the limbs of nearby trees. He walked back to his horse.

"Ain't you gonna bury 'em?" asked the rustler, mumbling the words. His lip was cut and swollen, he'd lost two teeth, and all but bitten his tongue in two. Never had he met a man with fists as quick and hard as the *vaquero*'s.

"What were their names?"

The rustler shook his head. He had refused to give Joaquin any information, not even his own handle.

Joaquin held out his hand so that the rustler could see the double eagles in his palm. "How many stolen Rimfire cattle did this buy?"

"I ain't tellin' you nothin', greaser."

Joaquin smiled. "You will."

He gathered up the reins of the rustler's horse and mounted his own pony. Rode a circle around the site, reading sign. There were the tracks he was looking for—Addicks and the man he had pursued. Joaquin followed them, trying not to worry. Addicks could take care of himself—couldn't he?

By noon Joaquin had found the spot, near the crest of a scrub-covered rise, where Addicks had fallen. He could not, of course, at first be certain that it was Addicks who had been shot, but he started fretting about it when he saw the blood on the rocky ground.

The sign was confusing. It took him a little while to decipher it. Two horses had come up this hill. One had gone down the other side into the gulch. A man had dismounted there, briefly, then remounted and headed west. A barefooted person—a woman by the size of the footprint—had ascended and then descended the hill three times. Joaquin followed her trail to the wagon trace, where close inspection revealed that a wagon had passed this way late yesterday, heading south. The woman had stopped the wagon, climbed the hill, returned to release the two mules in the traces, and then gone back up the hill again.

Later, a man had come from the south, riding one of the mules and leading the other. He too had clambered up the hill. Then both he and the woman had descended, leading a horse. They'd hitched up the mules to he wagon, tied the horse to the wagon's tailgate, and proceeded south in the wagon. The most telling clues were three spent shell casings from a Winchester repeating rifle, 44/40, on the crest of the hill, and some blood on the ground near the wagon trace.

Joaquin rolled a cigarette and pondered, trying to put the pieces together. The more he thought it over the more he worried that the blood he had found was Addicks Bell's. There had been some shooting up on the hill, that much was plain. So Addicks had finally caught up with the rustler. The man who had dismounted down there in the gulch had ridden off in a westerly direction. If that had been Addicks, why was he riding *away* from the Rimfire? The *vaquero* knew that his saddle partner carried a Winchester 44/40, but then so did many others.

Whatever the identity of the man who had been shot, it looked to Joaquin as though the man and the barefoot woman had found him and hauled him off. That gave the *vaquero* reason to hope that the man who had been shot was still alive, although there was no guarantee of this. They might have buried a dead man on the spot, or they could have carried the corpse somewhere so that it could be identified and given a decent burial. The blood near the trace was a good sign, though. Dead men didn't bleed like that.

"Hey, greaser," said the rustler, intruding on Joaquin's ruminations. "I want some water. I'm dyin' of thirst."

"*Como se llama?*"

"It'll be a cold day in hell 'fore I tell you my name."

Joaquin shrugged indifference. "Then it will be a cold day in hell before you get a drink of water from me."

"Bastard."

"*Sí.*"

"Did you lose your partner?" sneered the rustler. "Looks that way to me."

Joaquin ground the spent quirly under a bootheel and mounted up.

"If he's dead, so are you," said the *vaquero*, and began to follow the trail of the wagon, his prisoner in his wake.

When Addicks opened his eyes it took him a little while to clear his vision and focus on the rafters of the sod roof overhead. Shafts of dusty sunlight poured through more than a few holes up there. He was lying on a thin mattress adorning a rope slat bunk up against an adobe wall. He turned his head to scan the one and only room. A rickety table and a couple of benches, a rocking chair, a stone fireplace across the way. The room had the musty smell and derelict aspect of abandonment and decay. But someone lived here. There were curtains of blue calico on the two windows. An old quilt, folded, draped the rocking chair's ladder back. A Dutch oven was hanging in the hearth above a crackling fire. Whoever it was had precious few possessions.

The door creaked open on its leather hinges. Mattie took one step into the room, saw that his eyes were open, and whirled to run back outside. A moment later she was back with a paunchy, balding, red-faced man.

"You got some hard bark on you, son," said Liam. "I'll give you that. How d'you feel?"

It required tremendous effort on Addicks' part just to lift his hand to his chest. He felt the dressing which tightly bound his chest. Made it difficult to breathe, but then when he *did* take a breath his chest hurt like unholy hell.

"Water," he croaked. "Could use some water . . . "

"Mattie, fetch him a cup of water."

"Bring the whole river," said Addicks.

Liam scooted a bench over closer to the bunk and settled on it.

"You find me?"

"Nope. It was Mattie. She found you. Mattie's my daughter. You been shot, son. Bullet went clean through, though. You was plumb lucky. I'm surprised you ain't bled to death."

Addicks felt so weak he wondered if there was a drop of blood left in his veins. Mattie arrived with a tin cup full of water. She cradled his head in her arm and held the cup for him while he slurped greedily. A drink of water had never tasted so good to him.

"Obliged, miss," he said, when the water was gone.

She smiled, and Addicks wasn't so bad off that he didn't notice how pretty she was.

"So what happened, cowboy?" asked Liam. "Who ventilated you?"

"Rustler. I ride for the Rimfire."

"Figured as much, seein' that brand on your horse. Rustlers, you say?"

"Yeah. Somebody's been making off with our cattle."

"You don't say." Liam shook his head. "Cain't abide hideburners, myself."

"I could use another drink, ma'am," said Addicks.

Mattie crossed the room to the bucket of water near the fireplace, and dipped the cup into it. Addicks watched her all the way over and all the way back. Liam watched him.

"Who are you folks?" asked Addicks, finishing off another cup. "I don't recollect seeing you all around." Looking at Mattie, he added, "I'm sure I'd remember."

"Name's Liam. Liam Henshaw. This here's my daughter, Mattie, like I said. She cain't talk. Never has been able to. We just moved in here a few weeks back."

"Where from?"

"Missouri."

"Where is this place?"

"*This* place? Oh, it ain't too far from here Mattie found you."

"I reckon I owe you my life," Addicks told her.

"That you do," agreed Liam. "That you do."

"I'm wondering if you folks would do something else for me. They'll be fretting about me over at the Rimfire. Maybe you could take word that I'm still alive. Otherwise the whole outfit will be out looking for me."

Liam stared at him, blinked once, then cleared his throat.

"You reckon they'll be looking for you," he said.

Addicks nodded.

Liam stood up and took Mattie by the arm. "Cowboy, you get some rest. I've got to have a word with my daughter." And with that he all but dragged Mattie out of the soddy.

He walked some distance from the soddy, far enough that he could be sure Addicks wouldn't hear what he had to say.

"Jesus, Mattie!" he said, in a state of extreme agitation. "You've put me betwixt a rock and a hard place now. Don't you see what you've done, gal? Lord A'mighty, I shouldna let you talk me into bringing that range rider here."

Mattie stared, taken aback by her father's vehe-mence. Exasperated, Liam threw up his hands.

"Look, I didn't tell you this, on account of I didn't want you to fret none. But this here house and all is on Rimfire land. We're squatters, Mattie. You know what cattlemen do to squatters? If that young feller in there knew I was a squatter he'd shoot me quick as a settin' hen on a June bug."

She shook her head adamantly.

"Oh yes, he would," insisted Liam. "Don't go arguin' with me gal. Now we got to think of some-thing. Mebbe if he passes out we can put him back in the wagon and haul him off somewheres."

She shook her head even more violently than before.

"Now don't you go gettin' that look on your face, Mattie Henshaw. That's just like what your ma used to do when she was about to go mule-stubborn on me. We could put him somewheres where they'd be bound to find him. You heard what he said. The whole Rimfire outfit will be out huntin' for him. They'd find him soon enough. We could put him on the San Saba Road. Yeah, that's it. We'll take him over to the road and leave him there."

Hands on hips, she looked away and kept shaking her head.

Liam sighed. "Mattie, you're . . . "

He saw the two riders coming through the scrub oak, and felt a weight, anvil-heavy, in the pit of his stomach.

"Too late," he moaned. "Too late. I'm a dead man, sure as the turnin' of the earth."

12

"I am looking for my *compañero*," said Joaquin, sitting in his saddle and gazing steadily at Liam and Mattie. "He . . ."

"He's here," blurted Liam, staring at the Rimfire brand on the *vaquero*'s horse, looking at it as one might look at a coiled rattlesnake, and then he rubbed his throat, because suddenly he could feel the scratchy weight of a rope around his neck.

"Alive?"

"Yeah. We found him—well, my daughter Mattie did—a few miles north of here. He's been shot, but I reckon he'll pull through."

Joaquin did not immediately dismount, but from his vantage point surveyed the ramshackle soddy and the bluff rising behind it above the tops of the scrawny cottonwoods and sweetgums which told him that there was probably a spring somewhere near. Watching him, Liam felt his heart break into a gallop across his ribcage, and all his blood seemed to turn sluggish and cold in his veins, and he shuddered, wracked by a sudden and violent chill. Even the perspiration beading on his forehead was cold. Now the *vaquero* was looking at him again, him and Mattie, and Liam said to himself, his inner voice shrill with panic, *He knows! He knows this is Rimfire land. Which means he knows we're squatters.*

"*Mucho gracias*," said Joaquin, and stepped down off the horse.

"I reckon we saved your partner's life," gushed Liam.

Joaquin gave him a curious glance. "So it would seem." He turned to the other rider, and for the first time Liam noticed that the second rider's face was a bruised and bloodied and swollen mess. Joaquin drew the long-bladed belduque from the top of his boot and slashed the rope which held the man's ankles together beneath the horse's barrel.

"Get down," said Joaquin.

"Go to hell," croaked the hideburner.

Joaquin grabbed the offside stirrup and lifted. This sent the rustler head-first off the horse. With his hands bound he was unable to break his fall, and he landed so hard that it made Liam wince just to see it. The rustler rolled over on his back, wheezing and groaning at the same time, and looked up at Liam and Mattie.

"Water," he said. "I need water, for God's sakes. This bastard's tryin' to kill me."

"Rustler?" Liam asked Joaquin.

"*Sí*."

"Lookit what the sonuvabitch done to me!" whined the man on the ground.

"Watch your language in the presence of the lady, *amigo*," advised Joaquin, "or I will knock the rest of your teeth out."

"You stinking greaser. Your mama was a brown nigger whore."

Joaquin looked down at him with the mild revulsion of one who is examining something unpleasant which he has just scraped off the bottom of his boot. Then he turned abruptly to his horse and took his lasso, thirty-three feet of Brazos hard twist, from his rig. The rustler was struggling to his feet now; before he could react he found the loop around his shoulders, pinning his arms to his sides, and he tried to run, but Joaquin gave the rope a strong tug and put him on the ground again. The *vaquero* tossed the other end of the rope over a convenient and sufficiently stout cottonwood limb, caught it up and pulled. With a yelp the hideburner found himself lofted skyward. Getting him high enough so that his toes couldn't quite reach the ground, Joaquin tied the rope off around the trunk of the tree.

"Christ, I thought you was about to hang him," said Liam, and remembered to start breathing again.

"Maybe later. I would like to see my friend now. Maybe you could take the *caballos* down to the spring for me."

"I . . . " Liam realized that he was in no position to refuse. This was Rimfire land, which made that spring yonder a Rimfire spring bubbling up Rimfire water. He knew it, and he knew that this Mex cowboy knew it, so he nodded, and said, "I'll tend to 'em. Don't you fret."

Joaquin nodded and walked across the hardpack to the soddy and stepped inside like he owned the place.

Gathering up the reins, Liam held them out to Mattie. "Take these horses on down to the spring, gal."

Mattie shook her head and started for the soddy.

"Mattie!" roared Liam. "You come back here right this minute! You hear me, gal? Mattie! Dog-dammit, you better mind me . . . Mattie? . . . Now you're deaf as well as dumb? *Mattie!*"

Dumbfounded, Liam stared at the door through which his daughter had passed into the soddy and out of sight.

"Hey, mister," said the rustler. "Cut me down from here."

Liam turned and contemplated the man swinging by the rope from the limber cottonwood limb.

"Now why on earth would I want to go and do a fool thing like that?"

"I got money. I'll pay you."

"How much?"

"Hunnerd dollars."

"A hunnerd dollars?" Liam snorted. "You'd have

to pay me a lot more than a hunnerd dollars to cross that Rimfire bunch."

"Okay, okay. How's five hunnerd sound?"

"Five hunnerd? Dollars? American?"

"Yeah."

"Yankee dollars? None of them Confederate shin-plasters that's still floatin' around."

"Yankee money, dammit. Now cut me down!"

Liam pulled on his blue-bristled chin. Glanced at the soddy. Back at the man. Shook his head.

"Nope. If I did it, that Rimfire cowboy in yonder would like as not hang me from that tree in your place, only the rope would be around my neck. Nossir, I ain't got nothin' agin' you personally, mister. You want to rustle Rimfire cattle that's your business, and none of mine. But I ain't kept a whole skin for fifty-some years in this Godforsaken wilderness by sticking my nose in someplace it don't belong. So I'll just pass on . . . "

"Shuddup, you old windbag," rasped the exasperated rustler, "and cut me the hell down from here."

"Nope."

"You ought to be afraid of me and my pardners, friend, instead of that greaser. If you don't help me now by God I'll come back here and skin you alive."

"You? You're gonna do that?" Liam hawked and spit. "I don't reckon I'll see you agin'. Not this side of hell, anyroad."

He started through the trees toward the spring, leading the horses, as deaf to the rustler's curses as Mattie had been a few minutes earlier to his own orders.

Inside the soddy, Joaquin glanced over his shoulder at Mattie as she came in to stare suspiciously at him for a moment and then drift aimlessly over to the fireplace, across the room from the rope-slat bed where Addicks lay. There she stood, throwing sidelong glances across at Joaquin, who smiled as he hooked one of the benches at the table with his foot and dragged it nearer the bed and sat down.

"Looks like she thinks I might try to steal you away, *amigo*," he observed.

"What do you mean?"

"*Nada*. It isn't important. How do you feel?"

"I'd have to get better to die."

"You will live. But look at you. I should have known I couldn't leave you alone without you getting hurt."

Joaquin meant it as a joke, but Addicks was in no mood for jokes at his expense. He hurt too much.

"I did the best I could. Just because I wasn't born in this damned country and didn't cut my teeth on a gun barrel doesn't mean I can't do the job as well as the next man."

"Sorry. I didn't mean anything by it."

Addicks relented, and sighed. "No, I'm the one who should be sorry, Joaquin. It's just . . . well, I hurt like hell. I'm tired of lying here. But I don't even have the strength to sit up."

Joaquin nodded, sympathetic. "You will be down for a while. Tell me what happened."

"I chased him for miles. Then I came up over a rise and saw his horse down in a draw, didn't know he was hanging on the other side of that fool horse. Then he dropped off and the horse moved and he shot me before I could blink. What about you? Did you catch that other *hombre*?"

Again Joaquin nodded.

"You didn't kill him, did you?"

"No. I wanted to take him alive. I want the names of his *compadres*, and where we can find them."

"Has he talked?"

"Not yet," said the *vaquero*, and he did not have to add *But he will before I am through with him*, because his tone of voice told Addicks all he needed to know in that respect, and Addicks didn't bother asking him if he had even thought about turning his prisoner over to the sheriff in Lampasas. Addicks knew better. It didn't work that way out here. The sheriff was hired by the townfolks to keep the peace in the city limits. The cattlemen did not need him to keep the peace on the range. That was their job, and the Lampasas sheriff knew better than to interfere. On his own range the rancher made his own law, and his outfit enforced it.

Addicks didn't feel the least bit sorry for the rustler Joaquin had captured. He had lived in cow country long enough to have accepted the law of the range which said that a man fool enough to steal another man's livestock forsook all his rights—the right to a fair trial before an impartial judge and jury, for instance. The only reason Joaquin's prisoner hadn't stretched hemp was the information he had about the rest of the hideburners. He hadn't talked and he knew the only reason he was still alive was because he hadn't, just as he knew, as Addicks did, that when he finally did talk—and he would, Joaquin would see to it—he was finished. He was doomed unless he could escape. There would be no deals, no reprieve.

When Addicks had first come to cattle country he had thought the law of the range too severe, because he made the mistake outsiders usually made of weighing the loss of a few cows against the life of a man, no matter how much of a no-account the man was, and coming down in favor of the man. But he understood now that if a rancher let one man get away with stealing one cow then the word would get out and pretty soon he wouldn't have a steer left to his name, and cattle were his livelihood, and he could not let someone rob him of that, any more than a shopkeeper would let someone waltz into his she-bang and steal him blind without trying to stop it. The way Addicks looked at it now, any man who opted to take up nightriding and, by so doing, violate the law of the range, was choosing to die before his time, of his own free will volunteering himself to someday hang from a tree like a ghastly Christmas ornament.

"I am taking him back to Rimfire," said Joaquin. "Do you need anything, *amigo?*"

Addicks glanced across the room at Mattie, who looked quickly away. "No, I guess not."

"Then I will come and visit you when I can."

"I'll be up and around in a few days."

Joaquin chuckled. "Sure you will. And pigs fly. Stay out of trouble."

"What kind of trouble could I get into flat on my back like this?"

Joaquin nodded at Mattie. "The worst kind. Woman trouble."

Addicks felt his cheeks burning. "*Vamos*, you snake."

Joaquin left the soddy. Liam was just returning from the spring, where he had watered the horses.

"Everything okay?" asked Liam.

Joaquin gave him a long, speculative look that made Liam extremely uncomfortable. Without saying a word the *vaquero* spoke volumes, and Liam knew in that instance without having to ask what his obligations were.

"Don't worry about your friend," said Liam. "We'll take right good care of him."

"I know you will."

Joaquin cut his prisoner down, got him on his horse, tied him and rode away, touching the brim of his hat to Mattie, who stood watching in the doorway of the soddy.

"He knows," said Liam, as soon as Joaquin and his prisoner were out of sight in the *brasada*. He stood there in the hot sun, limp and lethargic in the aftermath of the tension which had stretched his nerves taut as brand new barbed wire, looking not at Mattie but at the scrub where the riders had disappeared. "He knows and he ain't gonna do nothin' about it as long as we take good care of his friend."

Then he turned to look at Mattie, but she had already vanished into the soddy.

13

When Joaquin blew in to the Rimfire Ranch on his clear-footed roan gelding, the men came from all points of the compass, curious about the *vaquero*'s prisoner. They came from the bunkhouse and from the breaking pen, where a fence-worming bronc was kicking up dust. It was midday, time for the noon meal, and Lopez, the old Mexican who had been the first man to ride for the brand, and who had been Big Sam's most trusted friend, was finished trying to poison the hired hands. As bad as his grub was, and as much as the men grumbled, not a soul on the payroll would have even considered suggesting that the Rimfire find a "belly cheater" whose stew didn't taste like the mud at the bottom of a buffalo wallow, and whose biscuits weren't so hard a man was likely to crack his molars on them. No, Lopez was a fixture at the Rimfire, and though they sometimes cursed him, the men all loved him like a father. And, besides, were he to go, and were someone who could actually boil water and make "dough-gods" you could actually chew commence to grub-slinging for the Rimfire outfit, what would the cowboys have to complain about? A range rider had to have something to gripe about or he just wasn't going to be truly happy, and so Lopez fit the bill nicely.

By the time Joaquin pulled up in front of the main house they were all there, all those who weren't out on the range—Monte and Lute and Bowdrie and McNeely and even old Lopez, his rheumy eyes blinking in the bright, slashing sunlight, his face walnut brown with a thousand deep creases, looking like old whang leather. He was small and bent. His hands were gnarled. But he still cast a big shadow, thought Joaquin. No one admired Lopez more than he. Lopez was truly an *hombre del campo*. No one knew more about cattle and horses and these *brasada* hills than Lopez, and while he was entirely too old to ride, his bones were too stiff for roping, and his vision too poor for accurate shooting, he was worth his weight in gold and then some for the wisdom he possessed—not just wisdom about the land and the livestock but after almost a century of watching people he usually knew what folks were going to do before they knew it themselves.

"Is this one of them?" asked Lute, squinting up at the half-dead rustler.

Joaquin nodded and stepped down out of his saddle.

"He looks some worse for wear," observed Bowdrie. "Did he give you much trouble, Joaquin?"

"*Poquito*. Not much."

"Where's Addicks?"

"Shot. But he will live."

"What the blue blazes happened?" asked Lute.

Joaquin told them the whole story.

"You mean he's laid up with squatters?" queried McNeely. He spat the last word out like it left a bad taste in his mouth, and Joaquin figured it probably did. No cowboy worth his salt had anything nice to say about a squatter. To him, a squatter was lower than dirt. Being either a sodbuster or cattle thief, and "feeding off" the ranch, he always meant trouble of some sort.

"We ought to go burn 'em out," growled Bowdrie.

"They saved our friend's life," said Joaquin.

It suddenly struck him how arrogant cowboys could be. That applied to him, too. He'd always considered himself a cut above a plowpusher or townsman. For the first time he asked himself why. A cowboy liked to think he was his own boss, the gallant knight of the open range, a free spirit living a free life. But that wasn't really true. A cowboy was just a hired hand. He worked someone else's stock and not a square inch of the range could he call his own. At least a granger could say he worked his own piece of land, and lived under his own roof, and had the pride of ownership. What could a cowboy call his own? His saddle, and sometimes, if he was lucky, a horse to put it on. Oh, he was free to come and go as he pleased, with no strings to tie him down. But that was a hollow freedom indeed, mused Joaquin.

"That don't make it right, them being here, does it?" asked Bowdrie.

"It gives them some rope, in my book."

"Let one stay and the next thing you know there'll be dozens of 'em swarming all over this range."

"I know," said the *vaquero*.

"It's snakes like thissun we should worry about, Bowdrie," said Lute, gesturing at the rustler. "You done for two of 'em, Joaquin. How many more you reckon there are out yonder?"

"A few more. Not many. But he won't talk. Not yet."

"Oh, he'll talk, I reckon," said Lute. "Once Yantis gets here."

"Who?"

"Mrs. Kenton told Lopez she's hired a man to come take care of our rustlin' problem."

Lopez was the main conduit of information between the big house and the bunkhouse. It had long been so. Sam Gunnison had always confided in the old *vaquero* and had come to rely on him to spread information through the rest of the outfit. Apart from cooking for the range riders, Lopez also did odd jobs around the big house, so it was only natural that Martha Kenton would turn to him and say "I have decided to do this. Tell the men." Just as her brother had done.

"Hired a man," murmured Joaquin. "What kind of man?"

"A professional," said Lute, in his usual, laconic, I-don't-give-a-hoot-if-the-sky-falls-in kind of way. It was important to Lute to appear as though nothing under the sun could shake him up. He was the type who would ride in off the range and tell you that every last Rimfire cow was cornbread dead with such a matter-of-fact delivery that you would wonder if you'd heard right.

"Yeah. A damned regulator," said Bowdrie, in his brusque manner. Bowdrie was the exact opposite of Lute. Seemed like Bowdrie never could keep his emotions from getting the best of him. He took everything that happened personally. If a train didn't run on time Bowdrie had to take a hard look at the situation to see if it didn't somehow adversely impact on his life, and if it did, then that proved there was a sinister conspiracy afoot with the object of making life miserable for him. Now, Bowdrie was at odds with this man Yantis, though they had never met, and though he probably had no idea, yet, why he should be.

"I heard of him before," remarked McNeely. "He's done most of his work up north. Montana and Wyoming, I think. Those big cattle associations up there hired him to clean out their hideburners. Rumor has it he cuts the ears off his victims. Turns 'em in for the bounty."

"So what's he doing down here?" wondered Monte.

"It's said he ain't too particular whose ears he turns in," replied McNeely. "Folks started to turn up missing—folks who didn't have nothing to do with rustling."

"She shouldn't have done it, you ask me," said a grimacing Bowdrie. "Hell, we don't need no help. Not that kind of help, for sure. Look here. Joaquin's done took care of half the problem already."

"I know one thing," said Monte. "Big Sam wouldn't like it. No, sir. He wouldn't like it not even one little bit. He'll be turning over in his grave, what with a man like Yantis stepping foot on his ground."

"My brother is dead. What he would or wouldn't like is of no consequence."

Martha Kenton spoke as she emerged from the house, looking sternly at the Rimfire riders. All but Joaquin were quick to take a strong and sudden interest in something else—the horizon, the toe of a boot, the antics of the bronc over in the breaking pen. And all of them, including the *vaquero*, swept hat from head.

"Perhaps Sam wouldn't approve," she said. "I can't help that. I must do what I think is best. If you don't cotton to it, I'm sorry. That's too bad. Running this ranch is my responsibility, until Emmy gets here. Believe me, gentlemen, when I tell you that I derive no satisfaction from this duty."

Standing there, hands on hips, chin raised in defiance, her eyes hard as polished blue stones, she reminded Joaquin of her brother. Not in size, of course—Martha Kenton was just a wisp of a woman, and Big Sam had been a brawny specimen, standing six-foot six in his stocking feet. And not in facial features, either—Big Sam's features had been craggy and coarse, while Martha's were aquiline, even delicate. No, it was in spirit that they so closely resembled one another. Just like her brother, Martha was the kind of person who made up her mind about something without wasting a lot of time chewing on it. And once her mind was made up, a six-horse hitch couldn't drag her off the mark.

She looked at the rustler, still sitting in his saddle, and then at Joaquin.

"Who is this man?" she asked.

Joaquin told her the same story he had relayed to the Rimfire cowboys moments before, and when he mentioned what had happened to Addicks Bell she nodded grimly.

"There's the reason I have sent for Mr. Yantis. You men are cowboys, not professional manhunters. I realize that you like to think of yourselves as fellows who are capable of dealing with any eventuality, but you must understand that while you are specialists at busting broncs and brush-popping steers, this problem calls for a specialist of another sort entirely. Were I to leave this problem to you, while I have no doubt you would resolve it in time, some of you would like as not get yourselves killed in the process. And I don't want that to happen."

"You fight fire with fire," said Joaquin, "and you still end up with a fire on your hands. It sounds to me like this hombre, Yantis, is his own brand of trouble. Hiring him, you trade one brand for another."

"It's been my experience that rumors of the sort which shadow Mr. Yantis are usually fabrications. Our neighbor, Mr. Wallace of the Spur Ranch, recommended him. We are fortunate that a man with the expertise of Mr. Yantis is available, and so near at hand. He is on his way from San Antonio, and should arrive here today or tomorrow. I'll expect all of you to stay out of his way and let him do his job."

Joaquin tilted his head in the direction of his prisoner. "What about him?"

"Lock him in the smokehouse. Give him some food and water. Then leave him for Mr. Yantis to deal with. He may have information concerning his colleagues that might be helpful."

"You are making a mistake, *Señora*."

The other Rimfire riders looked at him with admiration mixed with apprehension. They all felt as he did, but none had the nerve to speak out.

"It's not your place to question my decisions, Mr. Cruz."

Joaquin glanced at the other cowboys, and realized he would get no help from them. That didn't deter him. He didn't mind standing alone.

"We have a code out here," he told her. "A man fights his own fights. He doesn't hire someone else to do the job."

"Oh, yes," she said wryly. "Your code of the frontier. It's gotten a lot of good men killed. Needlessly."

She turned briskly and went back inside the house.

When the door closed, Lute let out a low whistle. "She shore raked her spurs over you, Joaquin."

Joaquin handed him the reins of the rustler's horse. "Put him in the smokehouse, like the *Señora* said."

The other cowboys accompanied Lute on his mission. Only Lopez lingered behind with Joaquin.

"I almost told her," said the young *vaquero*.

"It would have made no difference."

Joaquin nodded. Lopez was right. He always was. Aside from Emmy, the old *hombre del campo* was the only person left alive—now that Sam Gunnison was dead—who knew Joaquin's secret. It was the secret that tied Joaquin Cruz to the Rimfire in a bond stronger than that which inspired the loyalty of Lute or Addicks or even probably Shell Harper.

"She doesn't care about the Rimfire," said Joaquin. "She's just doing her duty. It's just a job to her. She said so herself. She can't wait until Emmy gets here, so that she can go home. I can hardly wait, either."

"It would do no good to tell her," said Lopez.

"Do you think she would even believe me if I did tell her?"

"People believe what they want to believe." The old man put a gnarled, much-scarred hand on Joaquin's broad shoulder. "What does it matter if others believe? It cannot change the fact that you belong to this land, just as the land belongs to you. If this is not true about you, it is not true about anyone."

"Does it belong to me, *anciano?* This land?"

"*Sí.* As much as it does to anyone else. Your blood and your sweat have nourished it, just as it has nourished you. But, most importantly, the bones of those who made you are lying within it."

Joaquin smiled fondly at the old *vaquero.* "Come on, and fix me a plate of whatever you stirred up for lunch. I'm so hungry I think I could actually eat your cooking."

Lopez flashed a toothless grin and chuckled, a dry, rasping sound. "You don't know it, but that's what keeps you alive. If you can survive my cooking, what on earth could kill you?"

The shots were spaced well apart, and as bad as the sound of the Sharps was, flaying Joaquin's nerves like a whip fashioned from red-hot strands of steel, the wait in-between was even worse.

Joaquin had never really thought of himself as a man toughened in body and spirit by the life he lived and the land he lived it on, but now he was given cause to wonder just how tough a man had to be to endure this with total and unfeigned equanimity. He glanced sidelong at the other men standing or sitting or leaning in the blue shade of the bunkhouse—sidelong, because he didn't want to make eye contact with any of the other Rimfire cowboys.

"Never thought I'd feel sorry for a damned rustler," muttered Monte.

Lute spat a yellow-brown stream of tobacco juice. His lean, weathered face looked like old whang leather in hue and texture, and it bore no mark of expression, but the passion behind the expectoration betrayed the strong emotion conjured up in his soul by the ordeal.

"I'druther hang than this," he said.

The shot came, a loud heavy deep-throated boom that rolled across the sun-hammered hardpack and the dusty, hot stillness and slapped them all in the face, and Joaquin saw them flinch, just as he flinched. Somehow that made him feel marginally better. He had endured dust storms and flash floods and hellish heat and bitter cold and hard drudgery and broken bones and rope-flayed hands and a knife wound and a gunshot wound and bad food and rattlesnakes and cholla spines and horse bite and bedbugs and bad water and even no water at all—endured it all without flinching, and really without thinking a whole lot about it, but this, this was something he wasn't sure he could handle.

"What piece of him did that bastard shoot off this time?" wondered Monte.

"His *cajones*, sounds like," said Lute, his tone phlegmatic, but his tobacco juice spit gave him away again.

Joaquin forced himself to look across the hard-pack. The rustler he had brought in was tied to a corral fence, his back to a post, spread-eagled, with his hands tied to two upper posts and his legs tied at the knees to two lower ones. He was howling now, an inhuman sound that made Joaquin's skin crawl. His face was covered with blood. So was his scrawny chest. He was straining ineffectually against the rope that held him, his head thrown back as he bayed to the white sun in the white Texas sky, and then his body convulsed forward, and he hung limp.

"Think he's dead?" asked Monte.

"I hope so," muttered Bowdrie.

Joaquin watched the man named Yantis reload the Sharps "Big Fifty" rifle and then walk up to the rustler and lift his head by the hair. He spat in the man's face. The man did not stir. Yantis strolled over to the horse trough and filled the bucket he had placed there earlier. He splashed the contents of the bucket on the man, who came awake spluttering like a half-drowned man.

The *vaquero's* eyes swept away from Yantis and the rustler, pausing briefly at the brass shell casings that littered the dust, winking in the sun, and he knew there were seven of them, though he could not count them at this distance. The seven shots were still ringing in his head. Yantis had shot off one of the rustler's ears, blown out a kneecap, blasted away a collarbone and nicked him a few times. But not his *cajones*. If he had, Joaquin figured the rustler would have come awake screaming. But there was a dark stain on one of the man's pants legs now. Either blood or the rustler had wet himself. Joaquin let his gaze swing on across to the porch of the big house, where Martha Kenton had just appeared.

"Cain't hardly believe she'd hire a man like Yantis," muttered Bowdrie. "She's got to have a heart of stone."

"Wonder does she think we can't handle the situation ourselves?" asked Monte.

"Well, we ain't handled it, have we?" countered Bowdrie.

"Big Sam would've," opined Lute.

"He was trying to when he got himself kilt," said McNeely. "I reckon Mrs. Kenton can hire anybody she's of a mind to. She's the big augur around here now. Leastways, till Shell gets back with Emmy Gunnison."

Joaquin's attention was drawn reluctantly back to Yantis, who was strolling in his unhurried, loose-jointed way back to the place where the shell casings winked in the tan dust, about forty paces from the corral fence where the rustler was crucified. A little too far for a short gun, mused the *vaquero*, and anyway it didn't look like Yantis was even carrying a charcoal-burner. He was dressed like a range rider: down-at-heel boots—spurless; the man made no sound when he moved—chaps, a faded blue shirt, a sweat-stained campaign hat. A bandolier was draped across his chest, the big 50/90 shells for the Sharps buffalo gun in the loops.

Yantis turned on his mark and raised the Sharps to his shoulder.

"I hear tell that Big Fifty can hit a target at five miles," remarked the lugubrious Lute.

Monte snorted. "You'd need a heap of salt to swallow that. Naw, but Dixon up at Adobe Wells hit a Comanch' buck at seven-eighths of a mile back at that '68 fight."

"If Yantis hits him square on, that bullet could go clean through him and the post too, I reckon," judged McNeely.

"'Twouldn't go through the post," said Bowdrie.

"Would too."

"I'll bet you a dollar it wouldn't."

"You ain't got a dollar. You spent it all last Saturday night at Belle's place, trying to cover every girl there."

"I got me a damned dollar," said McNeely, truculent, "and I'll fetch it if just to prove you a liar."

"Shut up," said Joaquin softly.

They shut up.

Yantis fired, the recoil jerking his shoulder back. The rustler uttered a guttural scream as the bullet blew a big bloody chunk of flesh off the leg above his one good knee.

"Judas Priest," muttered Monte.

Joaquin looked back at the big house. Martha Kenton had gone inside. *She'll fork out big money to pay a man like Yantis but she can't stomach the work she's paid for*, he thought. *She can't wash the blood off her hands any more than Pontius Pilate could, though.*

"Big Sam wouldn't stand for this," said Lute.

"No. He'd do it himself," said Monte.

"The hell he would. He was a hard man, but he wouldn't shoot a man to pieces. Would he, Joaquin?"

"Shut up," said the *vaquero*.

"Why have you got your hackles up?" asked Monte. "You worked that feller over purty good yourself, you know."

"*I won't waste any more ca'tridges*," Yantis shouted across the hardpack at the rustler—shouting to be heard over the man's wheezing sobs as he hung limply from the corral fence over a black stain of blood in the pale dust. "*Next one's right between the eyes.*"

"Lord, I hope so," prayed Bowdrie. "Put the poor bastard out of his misery."

Yantis plucked a shell from the bandolier and reloaded the Sharps.

"Awright!" screamed the rustler. "Awright, damn you!"

Broken, he began to cry.

Yantis walked up to him, lifted his head again by the hair. The men on the bunkhouse porch could not hear what the rustler said, but whatever it was it didn't take long to say, and Yantis was walking away.

"You bastard!" screamed the rustler. "You cold-blooded—"

Yantis whirled and fired.

The bullet struck right between the eyes and blew the back of the skull off and someone muttered a curse behind Joaquin as the blood and the bone sprayed and Bowdrie got up and stumbled urgently to the edge of the porch and vomited.

Joaquin watched Yantis coldly, without blinking. Yantis glanced towards the big house. Seeing no one there, he looked at the bunkhouse and then strolled over, the Sharps, now reloaded, cradled in his arm.

"You will want to plant him pretty quick," he said. "In this heat he'll get ripe in a hurry."

"You killed him, you bury him," said Joaquin, not bothering to conceal his hostility.

Yantis cocked his head slightly and smiled at the *vaquero* but the smile didn't reach his eyes, icy blue and piercing. His face was long and lantern-jawed, with a blue shadow of beard bristle on cheeks and chin.

"Leave him hang there then," he said, with complete indifference. "Buzzards gotta eat."

"I reckon he told you what you wanted to know," remarked Lute.

"Sure he did. You knew he would, didn't you?"

Lute almost spat tobacco juice, but with those glacier blue eyes on him he thought better of it. Yantis kept staring at him until Lute felt compelled to get up and walk to the end of the porch to stand near Bowdrie, who was sagging weak and spent against the bunkhouse wall. He spat, then turned and entered the bunkhouse, studiously avoiding Yantis' gaze.

The other Rimfire riders took their cue from Lute. Some walked away and others went inside. Only Joaquin remained, leaning against an upright. He rolled a cigarette. Yantis could see that his hands were quite steady.

"You don't like me being here, do you?" asked Yantis.

"You won't be here long."

"No, I won't. It won't take long to clean out this nest of vipers."

"How many?"

"Not too many. Don't worry. I can handle it."

"With that long gun you will not have to get in close," said Joaquin.

Yantis chuckled. It sounded like dry leaves skittering across old wood. "I'm a professional. I don't get paid if I get killed."

You are a coward, thought Joaquin. *A sadistic coward.* It came like a revelation to him, and where he had been afraid of Yantis before, now he was much less so. But he didn't say it. He figured he could cut Yantis down right here before Yantis could bring that Big Fifty into play, but there was no reason to, just because he loathed the man. He loathed him because he fairly reeked of the stench of death, but was that sufficient reason for killing? Joaquin decided it was not.

"Go do what you are paid to do," said the *vaquero*. "Don't let me keep you."

"Won't be nobody messing with Rimfire cattle when I'm through," said Yantis, turning away. "You can bank on that."

Joaquin watched him cross the hardpack towards the big house. Martha Kenton must have been at one of the windows, because she came out to stand at the door. *She doesn't mind hiring a man like Yantis but she doesn't want him to step foot inside the house and contaminate it with his presence*, mused Joaquin, eyes narrowed against the stinging swirl of gray cigarette smoke. Yantis and Martha conversed, and then Yantis walked to his buckskin horse, slid the Sharps into a fringed buckskin sheath, mounted up and rode away.

I'll be glad when Emmy gets here, thought Joaquin, the culmination of a jumble of uncharitable half-thoughts regarding Martha Kenton. Then he remembered Addicks Bell, or more precisely the squatter and his daughter, and an electric bolt of alarm shot through him. When Monte and Lute and Bowdrie and the others ventured out of the bunkhouse, as tentative as rabbits who have felt the shadow of the hawk emerging from their burrow, Joaquin was already in the corral catching up his horse. They started across to find out what he and Yantis had said to one another, but before they got there he was gone, riding west, heading for the soddy, and praying that he would get there before Yantis.

Because—since that man whose daughter had saved Addicks was the kind to borrow another's land, he would borrow another's livestock too when the mood struck him—Yantis would make no fine distinctions. Everyone in that soddy would become his prey.

15

Sitting in the box alongside the garrulous O'Hara, trying to see and breathe in the dun-colored cloud of dust kicked up by the six-horse hitch, baked by the sun atop a rollicking coach, Shell Harper endured one of the longest days of his life. It wasn't the dust or the sun so much, or even O'Hara, who had been talking unceasingly since Spanish Station, spinning one tall tale after another, but rather the fact that he would have much preferred riding inside the coach where he could look at Emmy. Not talk to her, or watch out for her, but just look at her. Seemed like that was all he wanted to do—had been ever since yesterday when she had arrived at Spanish Station. She sure beat looking at mile after mile of monotonous mesquite flats.

Sometimes the road to Killeen would dip down to a bridge or shallow ford across a creek where the willows and elms and sweetgum trees grew thick, and in that speckled blue-green shade they would find a refreshing coolness, but Shell couldn't enjoy these brief respites from the hammering sun and the choking dust because he was too busy watching out for an ambuscade.

Finally, the sun slid down the western sky and turned red as it melted into a layer of heat shimmer and the mare's tail clouds turned purple as they pin-wheeled across the sky.

"Yeah," drawled O'Hara, who wasn't anywhere close to running out of steam, even though he had been playing chin music all day, "my brother and me weren't atall alike. For one thing, I never could abide staying in one place too long, but he never stepped foot out of Dime Box, far as I know. I asked him once why he didn't like to travel and he said he didn't see any point in traveling, since he was already there. *Gee-up!*"

"This team," observed Shell, jumping into the breach as O'Hara took a breath, "is about bottomed out. How far to the next station?"

"That'd be Hollering Woman Creek. 'Bout a quarter-hour. Ain't that a funny name to pin on a creek? Now, I've heard tell it's on account of a woman whose kids were snatched up by the Comanch'. Nobody could console her, and she wandered up and down that creek for years, till the day she died, calling out for her little ones. She was touched, so folks just left her alone. They say her ghost still wanders them woods, and sometimes at night you can hear her calling out. I don't know about that. Jim Ketchum and his wife have been at the station going on a year now and they've never seen nor heard nothing out of the ordinary. Far as I know."

Shell didn't say anything. The reinsman cast a sidelong glance at him.

"Maybe I'm talking too much," he said. "It's just that I don't have company up here too often."

Shell sighed. "Doesn't bother me none," he lied.

"Now my brother, he's a preacher. So you can see how different we are, him and me. His problem is he gets carried away when he's up there in that pulpit, and goes to cussing a blue streak what would make a bullwhacker proud when he gets all worked up dish-ing out that fire and brimstone. So one day they were fixing to hang a couple of bad hombres, and the mayor asked my brother to say a prayer for the soon-to-be-departed, but he was worried on account of the way my brother cussed, 'cause when he got started the folks would laugh—they thought it was funny, you see—but a hanging was serious business, and the mayor didn't think it would be right to have folks laughing when two men were about to die, even two bad men. So the mayor wrote out the prayer for my brother, and he promised to read it just like it was written. The day came, and my brother climbed up onto the gallows and stood there in front of the whole county, with the two men behind him, standing on the trapdoors with the black hoods over their heads and the ropes around their necks. 'Bout that time he realized he'd left his spectacles at home, but he'd promised to read the prayer, and he couldn't hold up the hanging just to go home and fetch them, so he tried his best. But he couldn't make heads nor tails of the mayor's hen-scratchings. He couldn't see a stampede at ten paces without his spectacles. The harder he tried the madder he got, until finally he wadded the paper up and threw it at the mayor and said, 'Hell, Lou, I cain't read that goddamned thing so just hang the sons-of-bitches 'cause they're headed south anyway and a thousand amens won't do them a speck of good.' The whole town was laughing fit to be tied as they sprung those trapdoors."

The road from that point to Hollering Woman Creek was mercifully brief, and before long they were rolling into the yard in front of a dogtrot house whose better days had been long years ago. As he climbed the ribbons, O'Hara shouted, "*Hallo the house!*" The coach stopped, O'Hara set the brake and had one foot on top of the nearside front wheel, all set to jump to the ground, when he froze and threw a squinty-eyed look around and hallo'd the house again.

The place appeared to Shell to be deserted.

"Stay put," said O'Hara. "I'll check inside."

He climbed down and told the passengers in the coach to stay put too, then looked up at Shell. "Better toss me the scattergun, cowboy."

Shell held his Winchester ready as O'Hara walked up to the house, into the dogtrot, checking one side and then the other. He went to back of the dogtrot and looked down into the hollow where the creek danced over the rocks and an evening breeze rustled the tops of the trees. He returned to the coach shaking his head.

"It's a puzzlement. The horses are gone."

"And the Ketchums?"

"No sign of them either."

Shell looked around, sensing trouble, his nape hairs crawling. "I don't like it. Not one bit."

"No bloodstains. No bullet holes. No new ones, anyway. No sign of violence atall," said the jehu. "Jim and his wife must've just up and left. They didn't take much that I can tell. But then there weren't much here that didn't belong to the company."

"If they left on their own stick, they must've taken the horses, too."

"Yeah. Or someone else come along and took them." O'Hara rubbed a callused hand over his face, as though trying to remove the scowl plastered there. "If you'd told me Jim Ketchum stole company stock I wouldn't believe you. He and his wife struck me as pretty decent folk. But they're gone, and so are the horses, so I guess it's possible that I ain't near the judge of character I thought I was."

"I say we get out of here," said Shell. "It just doesn't feel right."

"The team's bottomed out. You said so yourself. We got to rest them. Give them water and graze, or we won't make it to the next swing station."

The coach door swung open and Billy Bishop came flying out, to land in a cloud of dust on the hardpack. Jack Ember stepped down, threw a sweeping glance about him, and then pinned O'Hara with his flinty gaze.

"What's the problem?"

O'Hara enlightened the Ranger. "The cowboy thinks we ought to move on."

Ember didn't even spare Shell a glance. "Were it a trap, they'd've sprung it by now."

Grissom was out now, looking down at Bishop in the dust with a strange look on his face. Bishop had rolled over and propped himself up on one elbow. He grinned, lopsided, at Grissom, and held out his hand.

"Help me up, kid."

Grissom started to reach out, but froze as Ember swung the Henry receiver down off his shoulder.

"I'd advise you to keep your hands off my prisoner, boy."

Grissom smiled tightly and walked away, stretching the kinks out of his back.

Killough stepped out of the coach and turned to help Emmy down. Brushing a wayward strand of chestnut hair out of her eyes, she looked up at the box searching for Shell, and smiled when she saw him. That smile did Shell's morale a whole lot of good. Last out of the coach was Teague. He consulted his Ingersoll stemwinder.

"Anybody got the right time?"

"It's suppertime, I know that much," said O'Hara. "I can tell it is 'cause my belt buckle is starting to scrape against spine."

"No, I mean the exact time."

Killough fished his own timepiece out of a coat pocket. "Half past six, Mr. Teague."

Teague checked his Ingersoll. "Thank you," he said. Pocketing the watch, he asked Shell to hand down the display case. That done, he waddled towards the dogtrot, struggling with his burden.

"I'm sure sorry Mrs. Ketchum ain't here to cook up some of her beans and biscuits," bemoaned O'Hara.

"Me, I cain't even boil water." He cast a sly and hope-ful glance in Emmy's direction, which Emmy was quick to decipher.

"I'll feed you, Mr. O'Hara. Don't worry."

He grinned so wide Shell was afraid his face would split in two. "Obliged, Miss Gunnison."

She started for the dogtrot, Killough following her. Ember hauled Bishop out of the dirt and gave him a hard shove in that direction. O'Hara proceeded to unhitch the team. Shell got down and helped him, although staying was still against his better judgment. They put the horses in the corral down by the creek, carried the harness up to the dogtrot and deposited it there. By the last shreds of daylight Shell studied the ground, trying to read the sign. But it yielded up no clues. O'Hara watched him, and every now and then sniffed the air. Smoke was curling out of the dogtrot's chimney, carrying an aroma of beans and blackstrap.

"You worried about the Bishop Gang?" he asked Shell.

"Aren't you?"

"Some. Not enough to put me off my feed. Aren't you hungry?"

Shell was scanning the trees for the hundredth time, listening to the chorus of the crickets down in the hollow, the sighs of the cooling wind in the tim-ber, the whicker of a horse down in the corral, the song of the creek. It was a nice, quiet, peaceful evening—and Shell didn't trust it.

"You go on. I'll stay out here for a spell."

"Well, I reckon it won't hurt to keep a lookout," begrudged the reinsman. "I'll take over for you after a while."

He went inside. Restless, Shell walked around the cabin and finally settled on the front porch steps. He watched the night fall, the shadows thicken. The air cooled and the earth seemed to sign in relief. He kept a hand on the rifle in his lap.

Emmy came out with a plate of food and a cup of coffee for him. She sat beside him on the rickety porch steps, so close he could feel the warmth of her body. Despite a long hard day of travel in dust and heat she smelled mighty good, the smell of a mountain meadow full of flowers basking in the sunlight right after a spring rain.

"Aren't you hungry?" she asked.

"I could eat."

"Well, eat then. I'll trade you." She handed him the cup and plate and took the Winchester out of his lap. "You eat and I'll stand guard."

He began to eat, in a desultory fashion at first, but after a few mouthfuls he realized just how hungry he was, and wolfed down the beans and blackstrap and the sourdough biscuit, then washed it all down with some good, strong java. Then he saw that Emmy was smiling at him. Her eyes were bright in the twilight.

"I'd forgotten what a pleasure it is for a woman to see a man enjoy her cooking."

"Guess you don't do much cooking up in St. Louis since your husband died."

She sighed. "No. I don't do much of anything, come to think of it. He left me well off."

"Why didn't you ever come home?"

"I didn't want to get into another argument with Father."

Shell shook his head. "I don't understand." He knew that Sam and Emmy had had a falling out which had resulted in her sudden departure, but no one knew the details. It had to have been something mighty severe to provoke Emmy that way, and force her to leave the Rimfire, because he was certain that she loved the place as passionately as her father had.

"I'm sorry, Shell. I didn't want to leave. But I had to. I couldn't stand it any longer."

"Stand what any longer?"

She looked at him with a grave expression on her face, and he shook his head.

"I know it's none of my business, Emmy. Forget I asked."

"Did you miss me?"

He looked at her sharply, taken aback by such a bold query, and wondering if she was toying with him. Years ago she had taken special delight in teasing him, or so it had seemed to him, and he thought she was up to her old tricks again, but much to his surprise she looked to be at least halfway serious.

"Well . . . " He gulped at the lump in his throat, then inched on out a little further on the limb. "Now that you mention it."

"I thought about you, Shell. Sometimes I thought about writing you. But . . . I never did."

"I wish you had," he muttered, way out at the end of the limb now.

"Is Joaquin still there at the Rimfire?"

"Did you think about him too?" Shell winced, mentally kicked himself. He'd just blurted it out, and now wished fervently that there was some way he could swallow up those hasty words. It was purely amazing, he thought ruefully, how quick jealousy could strike a man, and he hoped Emmy wouldn't pick up on it, but of course, being a woman, she did.

"Why Shell Harper . . . I do believe you're jealous."

"You sound pleased."

She was positively beaming. "Oh, I am. I won't deny it. Here." She gave him the rifle and took the plate and cup. "I'll bring you some more coffee."

She went back inside, leaving him there in the darkness, feeling elated and miserable at the same time. *Only a woman*, mused Shell, utterly mystified, *could turn a man every which way like that.*

16

By the time the men were fed, Emmy was too tired to have an appetite. She picked up all the plates and carried them to the kitchen. Killough offered to help, but she turned him down. In the kitchen, she looked back at the common room—at the gambler and the whiskey drummer, the Texas Ranger and the outlaw, the gun-toting kid out to make a name for himself and searching for recognition at almost any cost—and she was glad to be back in Texas.

Now she realized fully how dull and unfulfilling her life in St. Louis had been. All those years in the big house overlooking the Mississippi River, with fine jewelry and expensive gowns and house servants to wait on her hand and foot, the teas and the soirées and, of course, the opera—with all of that she had felt an uneasiness, a sense that she was wasting precious time, perhaps the best years of her life, cast in a role that did not suit her, and living in a world where she would never truly belong or be happy.

It had been a very long time since she had cooked and cleaned like this, but she really didn't mind. In fact, she kind of missed it. The novelty of having life handed to you on a silver platter was quick to wear off. She was tired, true. But at least she wasn't bored. And she had been bored to the point of distraction in St. Louis, bored with playing the lady.

"You look like you're lost in faraway thoughts, ma'am."

With a start she realized that Killough was standing there.

"I'm sorry," she said, with a nervous laugh. "I guess I was daydreaming."

"About St. Louis?"

He had asked her, in the coach, where she was coming from and where she was going, making polite conversation.

"Yes, I suppose so."

"Do you miss it?"

"No, not at all. On the contrary. I'm glad to be home."

"How did it happen that you went away?"

"I married a man who was the city engineer for St. Louis."

"An important job. You must have lived a good life."

"If by 'good life' you mean a nice house and lots of money and servants to cater to my every whim, then yes, I suppose I did."

Killough smiled. "But that's not how you would define a 'good life,' is it?"

"No."

"You never told me about your husband. Is he dead?"

"Mr. Killough, isn't that a rather personal question?"

"It would be, at a St. Louis soirée, wouldn't it? But those of us who live out here on the frontier are notorious for being blunt."

"Yes, he's been dead for over two years now."

"My sincerest condolences."

She shrugged. "He was a decent man. He loved me very much. Gave me a lot of nice things. Took good care of me."

"But you didn't love him. I beg your pardon. I like to think I am something of a hand at reading people. It's part of my stock in trade, after all. I usually know when a man's bluffing, when he's going to fold, or raise, or call me, or go for his gun, even before he himself knows what he's going to do."

"And what did you see when you read me?"

"A strong-willed woman who knows what she wants and won't let anything, or anyone, stand in her way of getting it."

"I don't know about that. But you're right about one thing, at least. I admit I didn't love him."

"Then why did you marry him?"

"I knew he would take care of me. I thought that was what I wanted. I felt . . . terribly alone. I'd left home, you see. I really shouldn't have done it. I ran away when I should have stood my ground and fought for what I thought was right. Instead, I tried to be somebody else, somebody I wasn't cut out to be. I guess I'm not making much sense, am I?"

"On the contrary. You're making perfect sense."

She smiled at him. "You're easy to talk to, Mr. Killough. You make a woman feel completely at ease. You make her feel as though she is quite safe in confiding in you. That's dangerous."

"I'm not trying to lure you down the road to ruin, Miss Gunnison. I just find you fascinating. You are quite different from all the women I've known, save one, perhaps."

"And you have known quite a few women, I'll wager."

"A good many, yes."

"No one special?"

His eyes grew dark and troubled. A shadow passed across his face, freezing the smile on his lips, turning it into a counterfeit smile, with no warmth, no meaning behind it, and Emmy realized, much to her dismay, that she had touched a raw nerve and hurt him, hurt him terribly, dredging up old memories with that innocent query.

"Once," he said, and his voice was hollow. "A good woman. Like you, ma'am. For a moment I thought I would have a decent life after all. But I was fooling myself. People have a remarkable capacity for doing that, don't they? She died. And life has held precious little joy for me ever since."

"I'm so sorry."

His smile was bleak, a brave try. "It happened long ago. I only think about her a hundred times a day, now, instead of a thousand. Most often at this time of day, when the sun goes down, and again very early in the morning. Do you think about your husband much?"

"I confess, not much."

"That why you don't use his name?"

"I suppose. It was all a big mistake. I knew it almost from the start. But I resolved to stay with him until he died. I felt as though I owed him that much. Tried to make him happy. And tried to fool him into thinking that I was perfectly happy, too."

"Did it work?"

"Oh yes. He was easily fooled. I . . . "

"Yes?"

"It's an awful thing to say, but when he died—he was aboard the sternwheeler *Virginia* when her boilers exploded—I thought for just an instant that God was being merciful—having mercy on me. Isn't that horrible? I'm ashamed to admit it. I don't know why I'm telling you all this, Mr. Killough. Things I never told anyone."

"Two years, and you're just now coming home?"

"I should have come sooner," she said, with self-reproach. "Then I would have been able to spend some time with my father."

Killough didn't ask her why she hadn't. He knew he didn't have to ask. Once the dam was broken there was no turning back the flood.

She sighed deeply. "But I wasn't brave enough. I was afraid it would not feel like home anymore. Then I would have to face the fact that I didn't belong anywhere."

"I know that feeling," said Killough, soft-spoken. "It isn't pleasant."

"But I was wrong. I'm not home yet, and yet I am. I know it hasn't changed. It never will. And I haven't changed either. This is where I belong. Always did belong, even when I was away. My father's dead, and I will grieve for a very long time, especially since we were never reconciled, but with all the sadness my heart is at peace."

"Such contentment is indeed a rare gift," said the gambler. "A sense of belonging is the most important thing of all. To a place, or to a person. I'm happy for you, ma'am."

"I feel as though we are old friends. You may as well call me Emmy. 'Ma'am' makes me feel old."

"Emmy, then."

"What about you? Is there no chance for you?"

"None. I've missed all my chances, to belong to either a place or another person. You have both."

"Both?"

"The Rimfire. And that cowboy out there."

"Oh." Emmy blushed furiously.

Killough laughed softly. "You should be honored. He would lay down his life for you."

"So would you."

"Of course. But it wouldn't be because I loved you. It would be something I would expect of myself, as I like to think of myself as a gentleman." *And it would be an easy choice to make, because I am tired of a life without love and without a home.* He did not have to say it—she already knew that part, instinctively.

"Oh, I don't know that he loves me," she said, a weak protest.

"Sure you do. Anyone with eyes can see it."

She thought back to those long-ago days, remembering herself as a young tomboy, and remembering how Shell Harper had awakened something inside her, making her aware for the first time in her life that she was a woman. Shell, who had been as wild and dangerous as a bronc, angry at the world without really knowing why, and determined to prove that he didn't need anybody, when all along that was just exactly what he needed most of all. Not once had he said a word to her to indicate how he felt about her, but it hadn't been necessary. His eyes betrayed him every time he looked her way. They still did. She'd known then, but in spite of that knowledge she had left him behind, along with every other facet of her past. The Rimfire, her father, and a cowboy who would die for her. She'd lost one of those things forever. The other two were hers for the taking. Killough was absolutely right about that.

Shell had changed in the years she'd been away, and all for the better. She'd always known somehow that he would turn out okay, even while most others shook their heads and opined that the boy's wild streak would take him down the wrong road to a bad end. Emmy had always been attracted to Shell, and now even more so, because the anger was gone. He was a tough, soft-spoken, self-reliant westerner. Her kind of man.

"Question is," said Killough, "do you love him?"

"Really, Mr. Killough. This may be the frontier, but surely some rules still apply."

"I am being forward. I apologize. But Mr. Harper seems like a decent fellow, for a cowboy, and he's certainly devoted to you. I'd hate to see you miss your chance. That's what I did, a long time ago, and I'm still paying for it. Most of the people I meet, I don't give a care what happens to them. But that's not the case with you, Emmy."

"Why such an interest in me? We've only just met."

"Perhaps because you remind me of . . . her." His smile was strained. "Well, I think I'll get another cup of coffee and then see if I can't talk Mr. Teague into a friendly game of cards." He started to turn away, paused, and added, "Tell that cowboy how you feel, ma'am. That's my advice, for what it's worth. You see, I didn't do that. I didn't tell her. I just rode away. I guess I just couldn't believe my luck. That someone like that could love me. Well, it didn't seem impossible. And by the time I'd come to my senses and went back to find her and tell her, it was too late. She was gone. Don't let that happen to you. Don't put it off until tomorrow. Tomorrow might be a whole new deck of cards."

17

When O'Hara relieved Shell, the Rimfire foreman entered the common room and had another cup of Emmy's coffee. Grissom sat slumped on a barrel near the window, alternating between gazing out at the moonlit night shadows and glowering at Killough. If the gambler was aware of Grissom's unfriendly looks, he didn't show it. Sitting at the roughhewn table in the center of the room he was idly shuffling a deck of Steamboat pasteboards. Shell watched his nimble fingers work. They seemed to have a life of their own as they cut, rifled, flipped, and shuffled the cards, at times faster than the eye could see. Killough was trying to get Teague interested in a quick game. The whiskey drummer sat across the table from the gambler with his heavy case against his leg. He seemed more interested in his Ingersoll timepiece than in poker, checking it twice, that Shell noticed, in a matter of minutes.

Billy Bishop sat in a corner watching everybody, a crooked smile on his lips, as though he knew a secret that no one else knew and which he would share in his own good time. Shell thought he looked mighty calm and collected for a man on his way to the gallows. But then maybe it was bravado. Shell had witnessed two

hangings in his lifetime. Both times the condemned
men had come across like Bishop was now—until they
felt the noose around their necks. Then the mask
crumbled. It would be the same with Bishop.

The Ranger, Jack Ember, sat at the end of the
table, away from Killough and Teague, the Henry
repeater on the table under his arm, and his body
turned so he could watch Bishop, and even when he
wasn't watching him, see him out of an eye corner. He
didn't look at anybody else, or talk to anyone either.
Shell wondered if the man had a family, or even any
friends. Maybe he didn't want any. He seemed a hard
and embittered man, and Shell speculated that perhaps
he'd had a family once, and lost it, and now all he had
left was the job. Pure speculation, true, but the fact
remained that Ember was a Texas Ranger, and
Rangers as a rule were men who weren't afraid to die.
That was what made them so dangerous, a special
breed of lawman. Shell did not know of a single
instance when a Texas Ranger had backed down from
a fight—all the more remarkable when one realized
that in almost every case the Ranger was outnumbered.

Emmy was washing dishes in a bucket, and Shell
walked over to stand near her. With seven people in
the room the conditions were rather cramped. The
door to the dogtrot was left open so that some of the
heat emanating from the White Oak stove in the corner could dissipate. She glanced up at him and
smiled, pushing a damp tendril of chestnut hair on
her forehead with the back of a hand. Shell had an
urge to reach out and help her with that errant strand,
but refrained, trying to rein in his emotions. He was
falling in love with her. Maybe he'd never fallen *out*
of love with her. Had he loved her, back in those dim-
remembered days? If so, it wasn't like this time. Back
then he'd been a confused, greenbroke kid who
wasn't sure what he wanted out of life. He was older
now, if not much wiser, and knew better what life had

to offer. One thing it seldom provided was a second chance. Another thing it seldom provided were women like Emmy Gunnison. Weary after many long days of travel, here she was feeding and cleaning up after a bunch of men, not because she felt she had to, but because she wanted to. That was the kind of person she was. Shell had never seen anyone like her and knew he never would again.

"Thanks for the supper, Emmy," he said. "Sure beats the chuck ol' Lopez cooks up."

She laughed. "Maybe I'll have to cook for you boys every now and then, just so you all don't starve to death."

"You're . . . you're going to stay this time, aren't you?"

"Yes." She was finished with the dishes, and dried her hands on an apron. "Are you going to stay, Shell?"

"If you are."

He saw then that he had gone too far out on the limb now. Emmy's smile faded. She looked troubled of a sudden, and looked down, around, anywhere but straight at him.

"Shell, I . . . I don't know how to . . . "

He decided abruptly that he didn't want to hear what she was about to say. Quelling the panic inside, he interrupted her, putting the cup of coffee down and moving away, saying, "I better take another look around. Excuse me."

Out on the dogtrot he took a deep breath and cursed himself for a gold-plated fool. O'Hara was on the steps with his scattergun. "All quiet," reported the reinsman. Shell didn't reply. He crossed the dogtrot and entered the other room. A strip of pale moonlight through the window provided just enough illumination for him to see by. A narrow iron four-poster bed, a dresser with a flaking mirror, a smaller rough-hewn table with a lamp on it—these were the room's furnishings. He shook the lamp, heard the kerosene jostle inside, and lit the wick with a strike-anywhere fished out of his shirt pocket. On impulse he checked the drawers of the dresser. A hand mirror and hair-brush lay atop a stained doily on the top of the dresser. The ivory handles were carved with the initials *HK*.

Shell heard a sound and turned to find O'Hara in the doorway.

"You're mighty edgy, cowboy," observed the jehu.

Shell tossed him the hairbrush. "If the Ketchums did pull out, they were traveling mighty light. I don't reckon that's company property, is it?"

"Helen," said O'Hara, seeing the initials.

"It doesn't look right to me."

"They just hauled their freight," said O'Hara, but this time he didn't sound quite so convinced. "That's the way with the folks you get working these stations, most times. Here today and gone tomorrow. Shoot, maybe that's the way with all of us, come to think of it. I've never put down any roots to speak of. I keep think-ing that someday I'll head on out to California just to see the Pacific Ocean. I know it looks pretty much like any other ocean, but I just got to see for myself. And a mountain looks like any other mountain, a town like any other town, a road like any other road. But we keep wandering anyway. You know what I mean."

"No. I have a home. The Rimfire."

O'Hara smiled. "Like my brother. 'Why travel when you're already there.'"

"Why did the Ketchums leave without their per-sonal belongings?"

"They stole the damned horses, that's why. They've got money on the hoof now, don't they?" O'Hara tossed the hairbrush back to him. "I thought they were pretty respectable folks, but I've been wrong before. If it had been Injuns there'd be sign. Besides, we haven't had Injun trouble on this road for a couple of years now."

Shell wasn't convinced, but there was no profit to be gained by debating the matter. "I reckon Emmy can sleep in here tonight."

"Sure," said O'Hara. "Us menfolks can bed down out here on the dogtrot or over in the other room."

Shell nodded and walked out. Grissom was on the dogtrot. He went to the back end, gave them a dark look, and jumped off into the weeds, traipsing into the trees down near the creek. O'Hara shook his head.

"Weren't for us being here, he would've made water right here on the dogtrot. Some people just don't have no shame."

Shell entered the common room and told Emmy about the sleeping arrangements.

"Good," she said. "I'm exhausted. Think I'll turn in." She started for the door. "Good night, gentlemen."

"Good night," said Teague.

"Evening, ma'am," said Killough.

At the door Emmy turned and looked at Shell. "Aren't you going to check under the bed?"

Shell grimaced, well aware that O'Hara and Killough were grinning at him, but making a point of not looking at them. Teague again consulted his Ingersoll.

"Already did," said the Rimfire foreman.

"Oh." Emmy blinked. The trace of mischief which had sparkled in her eyes a moment before flickered out. "Okay. Good night, then."

Shell went after her, caught her before she could close the door to what had once been the bedroom of Jim and Helen Ketchum.

"Emmy . . ."

"Yes?" She stood there with the soft lamplight casting a halo around her chestnut hair. Her eyes were bright, her lips slightly parted, as though she was waiting breathlessly for his next word. He wanted to kiss those lips, but he was afraid, afraid of seeing that troubled look on her face again.

"I . . . I just wanted to say good night."

"Are you going to sit outside my door all night long again?"

He nodded. "I reckon I will."

She almost said something—and this time he had a feeling it was something he *wanted* to hear. But she didn't say it.

"I'll see you in the morning," she said, with a soft, almost wistful smile, and gently closed the door.

Shell turned as O'Hara and Killough came out onto the dogtrot from the common room. The gambler was rolling a long nine between thumb and forefinger. Shell heard the tobacco crackling.

"Wish I worked for a boss as pretty as that," said O'Hara, and his smile told Shell he meant no offense by the comment.

Killough flicked a match to life and put the cigar between his teeth.

Two gunshots from inside the common room raked sharply across Shell's nerves. The one step he took toward the door behind Killough was reflex. Then a rifle spoke from somewhere out in the darkness and O'Hara grunted and was flung bodily into him, knocking him off his feet. Killough crouched, reaching under his brown broadcloth coat. A flurry of rifle fire from the darkness accompanied the angry whine of bullets in the dogtrot. Shell kicked the limp and heavy weight of the reinsman off his legs, scrambled up and hit the door to the bedroom with a bunched shoulder.

Emmy was standing there, frozen in the process of unbuttoning the white *camisa*.

"What . . . ?"

She had no time for more. Shell smashed the lamp with one swipe of his rifle's barrel, hooked an arm around her waist, and carried her onto the bed and over it and off the other side, landing with her on top of him, and in that way breaking her fall, because even in that moment he was thinking of her. They lay there, wedged in the narrow space between the bed and the wall.

Looking under the bed, Shell could see part of the dogtrot through the open door, and Killough's legs as the gambler took one long stride and then fell, spinning, to lie still.

"Hold your fire!"

It was Billy Bishop.

The rifles fell silent. Shell heard the thump of bootheels on the dogtrot. He saw muzzle flash as a gun spoke twice. Both bullets splintered the wall overhead. Then more thumping. The sound of horses at the gallop, coming closer, slowing, then galloping away.

"Shell," breathed Emmy.

"Ssh." He squirmed out from under her, raised himself slightly, and felt her warm breath on his neck.

A moment later she whispered, "Shell, what happened?"

"Stay down, Emmy. I'll find out."

18

Shell moved cautiously out onto the dogtrot, rifle ready, half-expecting to be greeted by a crash of gunfire. But there was none. He rolled O'Hara over. The reinsman was dead, and Shell closed the sightless eyes. Although he had scarcely known O'Hara, had only met him yesterday, the man's death was a shock to him. The reinsman had been that kind of gruff and hardy man who seemed indestructible. But death had come for him, sudden and quick—and from the back. Shell felt hot anger well up inside. He couldn't abide backshooters.

He thought the gambler was dead too, until Killough groaned and moved slightly. Closer inspection revealed that a bullet had entered his right side below the ribcage, at an angle, passing through the fleshy part and out the front. There was a lot of blood, but Shell figured he ought to live.

"You're lucky," he said.

"Funny," mumbled Killough. "I don't feel lucky." He was very pale. His eyes seemed partially glazed over, and his speech was slurred. Shell knew he had to plug those holes up pretty quick. But he had something else to attend to first.

"Hang on," he said, and entered the common room.

Ranger Jack Ember lay on his back, sprawled across his overturned chair. He had been shot through the head at close range. Bishop and Teague were gone, of course. Teague's big case was open on the floor. A rack containing bottles of Kentucky bourbon had been lifted out of the case to reveal a hidden compartment in the bottom. The compartment was empty now, but Shell had a hunch about what it had previously contained—the gun Teague had used to kill Jack Ember.

The Ranger hadn't had a chance. Teague had caught him completely by surprise. Who would have suspected a paunchy, bumbling, inoffensive whiskey drummer? Shell remembered how Teague had been continually checking his watch. So this had been planned down to the last detail. Clearly, the Bishop Gang had done away with the station keeper and his wife, as well as the horses. Were the Ketchums alive or dead? With these desperadoes, Shell decided it had to be the latter. Just as clearly, the plan had been for Teague to make his move whenever a favorable moment presented itself, anytime after a certain prearranged hour, at which time Teague could be assured that his compatriots were in place out in the darkness. The favorable moment had come when Killough and O'Hara left the common room, after Shell had followed Emmy out and Grissom had gone into the trees to relieve himself. That left Teague alone with Billy Bishop and the Texas Ranger.

Shell noticed that the shackles Bishop had worn were on the floor beside Ember's corpse. And the Ranger's Henry repeater was missing. Teague had killed Ember, rifled his pockets for the key and unshackled Bishop, who had taken the Henry as he and Teague made a break for it.

Shell nodded grimly. A damned clever plan. Ever since Spanish Station he'd been expecting the Bishop Gang to hit the stage in a straightforward, guns-blazing manner. But no, they'd been smarter than that. A lot smarter.

Confident now that Bishop and his hellions were long gone, Shell returned to the dogtrot. Emmy was bending over Killough, who was losing consciousness.

"I thought I told you . . . " started Shell, annoyed that Emmy was out here in the open, in harm's way, against his orders, because even though the Bishop Gang was at least a mile away by now there was still Buckhorn's hired gun, Pratt, to worry about.

But she didn't let him finish scolding her. "We've got to cauterize these wounds, and quickly. Help me carry him inside."

Shell took one step and then whirled in a spinning crouch, raising the Winchester.

Grissom stood, pasty-faced, at the steps. He jerked back and threw his hands up.

"Don't shoot!" he cried.

Shell relaxed, but not much—and he didn't lower the rifle.

"You missed the show," he said.

"I . . . I was out in the woods. I heard the shooting and . . . "

"Well, it's all clear now," said Shell coldly. He lowered the rifle. "Help me carry Killough inside."

Grissom took the gambler by the legs and Shell, handing the Winchester to Emmy, took the arms. A low, ragged groan escaped Killough's lips as they picked him up. The gambler passed out. They carried him into the common room and laid him on the table. A determined look on her face, Emmy tossed the rifle back to Shell and went to Killough, ripping his bloody shirt open.

"I'll need hot water, and the sheets off that bed in the other room," she said.

Shell took the coffeepot out and poured the dregs of the overcooked crank it contained into the weeds at the back end of the dogtrot. He detoured into the bedroom and fetched the sheets, and coerced water from the pump. Emmy tore the sheet into strips as the water heated on the White Oak stove. She washed the wound. Taking one of the bottles from Teague's case, she poured whiskey on the blade of a knife from the kitchen and laid the knife on top of the stove. Drenching the bulletholes with whiskey, she shook her head at the blood. It was still coming. She looked at Shell. There was a puddle of blood under the table. Her hands were stained with it. Shell nodded and fetched the knife, wrapping one of the bedsheet strips around the handle to keep from burning his hand.

"I'll do it," he said.

"No." Emmy took the knife and laid the blade against one of the bulletholes.

The stench of burnt flesh reached Grissom's nostrils. Stomach churning, he turned quickly away.

Emmy cauterized the other bullethole. The bleeding was stopped. She said a silent prayer and used a long strip torn from the bedsheet as a dressing. When finally she was finished she glanced again at Shell and saw the unabashed admiration on his face.

"You're a helluva woman, Emmy."

Her smile was tired. She tried to brush a stray tendril out of her eyes with the back of a bloodstained hand. This time he didn't hesitate, and did it for her.

"Thanks," she said.

"Any time."

She looked at Killough. "I think he'll make it. But he'll have to stay here for a spell. He could start bleeding again."

"Can we move him into the other room?"

She nodded. "I think that would be all right."

"Grissom. If you're going to be sick, do it outside. Otherwise, help me carry him."

"I'm okay," muttered Grissom, and took the gambler's legs again.

They laid him out on the bed. Shell retrieved the

lamp from the floor. The chimney had been shattered, but the base still contained a little kerosene, and he lit the lamp and left it burning low on the bedside table. He covered Killough with an old faded quilt and turned to discover that Grissom had left the room. Shell crossed the dogtrot to the common room. Emmy was sitting at the table looking blankly at the body of Jack Ember.

"Where's Grissom?" he asked.

"I thought he was with you."

"He'll probably steal a horse and light out." He laid a hand on her shoulder. "Are you okay?"

"I'm fine. What happened here, Shell?"

"It was Teague. He's one of Billy Bishop's boys. The rest of them were waiting out in the night for him to make his play. The Ranger didn't have a prayer. O'Hara, either. They backshot O'Hara, Emmy."

She shook her head. "It all happened so quickly . . . "

"Usually does."

"What are we going to do now?"

"There won't be another stage through for a week. Maybe somebody will come along sooner. I don't know. We can't move Killough, and the nearest sawbones is probably Killeen. That's almost a day's ride. But I'm not sure Killough needs a doctor any more. What could a doctor do that you haven't already done for him? You haven't lost your touch, Emmy."

"I grew up nursing a whole outfit of accident-prone cowboys, remember?"

"I remember when I broke my fool arm trying to bust a bronc. We could take two of the horses and ride on, you and me. But that would mean leaving Killough."

"Meanwhile," she said, "Billy Bishop is getting away."

"You're still alive, and that's the main thing. Bishop isn't our problem."

She stood and turned on him. "What do you

mean it isn't our problem? Look at that man." She pointed at Jack Ember. "That's a Texas Ranger lying there."

"Emmy, I'm sorry as all get-out that he got killed, but that's the risk he took when he started wearing that badge."

"Shell!"

"Dammit, Emmy. My job's to get you back to the Rimfire safe and sound. I'm not a lawman. I've got enough to worry about with this man Pratt."

"Bishop *is* our problem," she insisted. "As long as he's on the loose he's every law-abiding Texan's problem. And I for one do not intend to sit here and do nothing."

Steel just gaped at her.

"Emmy," he said, getting frantic now, "what can the two of us do against a gang of desperate men?"

"We'll do whatever we have to do."

"Be reasonable . . . "

Her eyes narrowed and flashed, and Shell braced himself, because he saw the storm coming.

"I *am* being reasonable. And if I have to I'll go after Bishop myself . . . *what are you grinning at?*"

"You." He shook his head in pure wonder. "Lord, Emmy. You're one of a kind. And it's funny, but what you said about Bishop being every Texan's problem—I made the same argument in Spanish Station, trying to persuade Ember to let us ride that stage. Now I wish I hadn't."

"So you'll ride with me."

"I'm going where you're going, so if you're going after Billy Bishop and his boys then I guess I am, too. But what about Killough?"

"I'll look out for him," said Grissom, standing in the doorway.

"I thought you'd lit a shuck," admitted Shell.

"I thought about it. But I'll stay, until someone else comes along, or he's able to fend for himself."

"Doesn't make much sense to me," said Shell. "Why would you care if Killough lives or dies?"

"Shell, don't," said Emmy, touching his arm.

"I ain't surprised you don't trust me," said Grissom solemnly. "But I'll stick. You have my word on it. Now maybe my word ain't much good these days. Never has been. But that's gonna change."

"Your word's good enough for us," said Emmy.

Shell wasn't sure if it was good enough for him, but he didn't contradict her.

Grissom nodded, turned to leave, then looked back at them. "Until tonight, I thought I wanted to be like Billy Bishop. I . . . I thought that way folks would have to notice me. As it stands, nobody cares if I'm even alive. But I see now that I was wrong. I don't want to be like Bishop anymore."

When he was gone, Shell said, "Well, I'll be."

At first light Grissom and Shell dug two graves. When they were done, and O'Hara and Jack Ember were laid to rest, Emmy emerged with a Bible she had been carrying in one of her valises, and read from Psalms.

"'The Lord is my shepherd; I shall not want. He maketh me to lie down in green pastures: He leadeth me beside the still waters. He restoreth my soul . . .'"

Shell's gaze drifted across Hollering Woman Creek, into the woods, and he wondered where the bodies of Jim Ketchum and his wife lay. Today the buzzards would come and point the way, and Grissom would have two more graves to dig.

"'Yea, though I walk through the valley of the shadow of death, I will fear no evil: for thou art with me . . .'"

His thoughts wandered to that day not long past when they had buried Sam Gunnison. Of late there had been too much dying, and it seemed likely there would be more right soon, since Emmy was bound and determined to chase Billy Bishop and bring him to justice. *She ought to say a prayer for us while she's at it, because it'll be a miracle if we aren't both killed.*

"'Surely goodness and mercy shall follow me all the days of my life: and I shall dwell in the house of the Lord for ever.' Amen."

Shell went to the corral and brought up two of the horses. Grissom was sitting on the porch steps, whittling a stick. The Rimfire foreman walked into the bedroom, where Emmy was checking on Killough one last time. The gambler was conscious.

"Miss Gunnison tells me the two of you are going after Bishop."

Shell grimaced. "Looks that way."

"Wish I could ride along. But I don't think I'll be going anywhere for a spell."

"Mr. Grissom is staying here with you," says Emmy. "He'll look out for you until help comes along."

"On the other hand," said Shell, "he might just steal you blind and be on his merry way."

"Now, Shell," said Emmy, admonishing him.

"Maybe I'll teach him how to play poker," said Killough. "I wish you both good luck, but I have a feeling that against the two of you it's Billy Bishop who will need all the luck he can get."

They were riding away from the dogtrot, bareback on the two stage-company horses, when Emmy said, "You know, I think Mr. Killough is right."

"It occurred to me," replied Shell dryly, "that we were so busy with those bulletholes we forgot to check him for a head injury."

19

On his way to the remote soddy where Addicks Bell lay recuperating in the tender care of the girl named Mattie, Joaquin Cruz stumbled across something he later wished he had never seen. A single rifle shot drew him to a hollow encompassed by *brasada* hills. Down in the hollow lay a gaunt longhorn. Kneeling over it, knife in hand, was a lone man. Joaquin recognized him immediately.

Mattie's father.

Liam seemed to feel the *vaquero*'s eyes on him, for he cast a shifty, anxious look over his shoulder. But he did not see Joaquin. The Rimfire rider and his horse were concealed by the brush. The squatter went back to work, skinning the longhorn. He spread out the hide and proceeded to carve the choicest cuts off the fresh carcass. A swayback mule stood patiently nearby. An old percussion single-shot rifle lay on the ground next to Liam. Joaquin wondered if the man had reloaded after killing the steer. Then the *vaquero* decided it didn't matter if the rifle was loaded or not. He touched his mount with his spurs and rode on down out of the scrub.

When Liam heard the horse he looked around and let out a yelp at sight of the Rimfire man. Blind with panic, he reached for his rifle, but when a pistol appeared as though by magic in Joaquin's hand he changed his mind and decided to make a run for it. In his haste he tripped over the dead longhorn's hind legs and sprawled. Scrambling to his feet, he made for the brush, ignoring the mule. Liam wasn't all that bright but he was smart enough to know he couldn't outrace Joaquin on that old knobhead. The mule had two speeds, a plodding walk and standing still. He thought his only chance was to try to lose the Rimfire rider in the *brasada*. The brush was so thick in places that a man, were he able to crawl deep enough into it, could escape detection.

But he didn't get anywhere near the brush.

Joaquin kicked his horse into a gallop. He had the pistol holstered and his lasso shaken out and twirling in the air over his head in no time at all. The flick of a nimble wrist and the loop settled neatly around Liam's shoulders. Joaquin dallied the other end of the hard twist around the apple of his saddle and checked his cowpony. The horse abruptly stopped, sitting back on its haunches. The rope sang taut and Liam's legs ran out from under him. The *vaquero* dismounted. The cowpony backstepped, keeping the tension on the rope, so that when Liam tried to get up he was jerked off balance and sprawled in the dust again. As Joaquin's shadow fell across him he lay suddenly very still.

"Don't kill me!" he cried. "For Chrissakes, don't kill me! You . . . you wouldn't leave my daughter all alone a poor orphan in this cruel world with nobody to look out for her . . . would you?"

"She would be better off, I think." Joaquin laid a hand on his pistol.

"Oh Gawd!" squawked Liam, cringing, squeezing his eyes shut, and shaking like a leaf in a hurricane.

"Get up," said the *vaquero*. He did not draw the gun, but rather grabbed the taut lariat. When he did, the horse stopped backstepping.

Liam squirmed on the ground, as though he were being struck by invisible bullets.

Impatient, Joaquin nudged him with the toe of his boot. "Get up pronto, or I *will* shoot you."

Liam managed to get to his knees. There he remained, hands clasped together, in an attitude of prayer. "Please don't kill me," he sobbed. "I'll . . . I'll give you anything you want, just . . . "

"Quiet!" rasped Joaquin. "You don't have anything to give. You are a thief. You live on stolen land, in a stolen house, and you eat stolen food. But worse than that, you are a coward. Now get up!"

Liam struggled to his feet. "What are you going to do to me?" He vividly remembered the condition of the rustler this man had captured a few days ago.

"Finish what you started."

"Huh?"

Joaquin gestured curtly at the half-butchered steer. "Finish it."

Leery, perplexed, and so afraid he could scarcely keep from soiling himself, Liam worked his way out of the lasso. He had dropped the knife. He searched for it in the sparse grass, found it, stooped to pick it up. Joaquin's hand remained on the butt of his pistol, knowing that if he dropped his guard Liam would try to use that blade on him. Cowards were more dangerous than brave men.

"Go on," prompted the *vaquero*.

"We saved your friend's life, remember. My daughter and me did."

"I remember. Why do you think you're still alive?"

Liam returned to his work on the steer. When he was done, he tied the hide up into a bundle, hair side out, using a short length of rope. This he secured to the pommel of the old henskin the mule was wearing.

"What's gonna happen to me?" he asked.

"You're lucky. A man named Yantis is somewhere

in these hills. His job is to rid the Rimfire of rustlers. If he had found you, you would be dead. Yantis doesn't take prisoners. And he's being paid by the head. Or rather, by the ear. They say he cuts the ears off his victims and turns them in for his bounty. Just like wolf hunters do."

"It ain't me I'm worried about. It's Mattie."

Joaquin didn't buy that. "You lie. Get on the mule. *Andale.* If you try to get away I will shoot you. Do you believe me?"

Liam nodded.

"Bueno. Es verdad."

Liam knew it was true. As roughly as he had treated that rustler, this man was capable of doing worse.

Mounted, they rode west, heading for the soddy, Liam in the lead and Joaquin right behind.

Mattie came to the door as they rode up to the soddy. She watched impassively as Liam and Joaquin dismounted, and read the situation correctly. Her father's expression spoke volumes.

"Joaquin!" Addicks was pleased to see his friend, but his grin was quick to fade as the *vaquero* gave Liam a hard shove towards the table and ordered him to sit down. Liam did as he was told. Now that it looked as though he wasn't going to die after all, the squatter was becoming increasingly truculent. He was a man with precious little pride, but he did not like being manhandled and humiliated in the presence of his daughter. As for Mattie, she stood with her back to the wall, just inside the door, with her arms folded and a stricken expression on her face. Joaquin did not fail to notice that she had washed her face and brushed out her hair. She was indeed a very attractive young woman, and she was taking pains to appear so, and Joaquin thought he knew why. She wanted to look her best for Addicks.

"What's going on here?" asked the object of her affection. "What's wrong, Joaquin?"

"*Señora* Kenton has hired a man called Yantis. He is a regulator."

Addicks looked a lot better than he had a few days ago, thought Joaquin. He had some color back. The girl was taking good care of him. Addicks' book of Shakespeare lay open beside him on the bed, and Addicks wore his spectacles. Joaquin surmised that his friend had been reading to Mattie. Addicks derived a great deal of pleasure in sharing his love of literature with others. But now Shakespeare was forgotten—and Addicks did not look at all pleased. He had taken the morsel of information provided by Joaquin and deduced the rest.

"The rustlers," he said. "Why did she do that? That's not the way we handle these things."

"You are not safe here, *amigo*."

"Me? Why? Because of Yantis? I don't . . . "

He looked at Liam. Then at Mattie. Finally back to Joaquin. Reading their faces, he knew the truth of it. Watching him closely, Joaquin could see this, and nodded.

"I caught this one butchering a Rimfire steer," said the *vaquero*.

Addicks looked away. Joaquin felt sorry for him. Something had developed between his friend and the girl, Mattie. The *vaquero* could feel it, an electricity in the air, and he knew that despite the pain Addicks was suffering he had enjoyed his brief stay here in her care. But now, suddenly, the idyll was over, shattered, and the bond between the two of them was in jeopardy.

"What's one steer?" said Addicks, bitterly.

Joaquin was startled. That was the last thing he thought he would hear from any man who rode for the Rimfire, and the remark alerted him to the fact that Addicks' loyalty to the ranch was being supplanted by another kind of loyalty, born of an emotion which, since Adam, had blinded man to the cold, hard, brutal realities of life.

"You know better than that," snapped Joaquin. "You let one squatter in and the next time you turn around there will be twenty. And they will all be butchering your cattle."

"But what's one steer when we've got . . . well, how many do we have, Joaquin? Do you know? How many thousands wear the Rimfire brand? Five thousand? Six? Ten thousand? What's one miserable steer?"

"You would not have said this a few days ago."

"Maybe I'm smarter than I was a few days ago."

"No, you're not. I'm taking you back to the ranch." Joaquin turned to Liam. "I'll need the use of your wagon."

He wasn't asking permission, so Liam didn't say anything.

"What about them?" asked Addicks.

"What *about* them? Once they're off Rimfire range, they won't have to worry about Yantis."

"Joaquin, they saved my life."

Joaquin glanced at Mattie, then back at Addicks. His expression did not soften.

"Because of that, I did not shoot him. Because of that, he is free to go. That is all I owe them."

"It isn't right," insisted Addicks. "Just because you ride for Rimfire doesn't make you God. They're not hurting anything or anybody staying here. They need a place to live, and this soddy is available. And one or two or even a hundred of our cows don't make a bit of difference in the grand scheme of things."

"If you really believe that, why did you take on those rustlers? Why did you get shot? Why didn't we just let them steal those cattle?"

"That's different."

"There is only one difference." Joaquin pointed at Mattie, the way a prosecutor in a court of law would point at the guilty party. "Her."

Jaws clenched, Addicks said, "I'm not going any-where."

"Yes, you are."

"No, I'm not. I quit."

Joaquin was stunned. "You don't mean that."

"Every word. I don't ride for Rimfire anymore, not if it means poor folks like this have to go without food, or a roof over their heads."

The *vaquero* laughed. He knew it was ill-advised to do so, and he saw the anger darken Addicks' face. But he couldn't help it. "They don't *have* to." He gestured sharply at Liam. "Look at this man. Has he ever worked an honest day in his life? No. Why should he? He takes what belongs to others. What others have worked and bled and died for. He is a thief, just like the man who shot you, and there is no difference between them."

"You might as well *vamos*," said Addicks stiffly.

Joaquin shook his head, frustrated. He could see that Addicks had made up his mind to be a fool, and no amount of chin music was going to change it.

"If you weren't gunshot, I would drag you back," said the *vaquero*.

"You could try."

Joaquin turned on his heel and walked to the door. He paused, looked sharply at Mattie. She looked down at the ground, and the *vaquero*, heavy of heart, glanced back at Addicks.

"Yantis will kill you all."

"Maybe so," said Addicks. "But he'll know he's been in a fight when it's over."

Without another word, Joaquin left the soddy.

20

Liam Henshaw stood at the soddy's window and watched Joaquin ride away. He waited until the Rimfire *vaquero* had disappeared into the *brasada* before turning to bark a curt command to Mattie.

"Gather up all our possibles, gal, while I hitch up the mules."

"You'd better stay," said Addicks.

"Stay? You must have a fever, cowboy. You've plumb lost your mind. Didn't you hear what your *amigo* said? There's a regulator out there somewheres who won't think twice 'bout takin' my ears for bounty, nor my daughter's."

"You'll be safer here."

Liam snorted at that. "Yeah, right. If the regulator don't kill me then your Rimfire boys can ride in and shoot me."

"They wouldn't do that."

"How come they wouldn't? On account of you? I seem to recollect you don't ride for the Rimfire no more."

"Still, they wouldn't go through me to get to you."

"Oh, well, ain't that grand? I'm just as safe and sound as I can be, long as you're around. Is that it?" Liam snorted again. "I've had nothing but trouble ever since I laid eyes on you, cowboy. We should've left you out there in the brush where we found you."

Mattie had moved to the bedside. Now she stamped her foot, pointed at Liam, and then placed a hand over her mouth. Her movements were sharp with anger, her eyes flashing.

"I will not shut up!" yelled Liam, irate. "Now, you do what I tell you. We're making tracks."

He stormed out of the soddy.

Addicks looked up at Mattie, but she wouldn't meet his gaze. With a stricken expression, she turned away.

"Mattie."

She stopped, head down, still not looking at him.

"Mattie, look at me."

She looked at him, and he saw the silent tears, and they wrenched at his heart. He knew then that he could not allow her simply to walk out of his life. If she left, she would take all the light and warmth and hope and laughter with her, and those things would be gone from his life forever—he would never get them back. Never again would the tranquil beauty of a sunrise hold any allure for him, or the words of his precious books have any meaning, or his future any promise. He had never before given much thought to loneliness, having always enjoyed solitude, but he would never enjoy it again. Now he could not even remember much about his life prior to meeting Mattie. None of it seemed to matter. He had known her for a matter of days, yet he was completely and irrevocably changed.

"Don't go," he said, and held out his hand.

She hesitated to take it. Somehow Addicks knew that if she didn't he would lose her forever.

"Mattie, please. Don't go. Stay with me. I . . . I know I'm asking a lot—asking you to leave your father. I guess I've got no right to do that. But I just can't let you go."

Still she did not take his hand. The tears continued to stream down her cheeks.

"Mattie," he said, his voice hoarse with emotion, "I don't want to lose you." It was all he could think to say. It was reduced to that. He wanted to inundate her with good solid reasons for her to stay with him, a barrage of unassailable logic which could not fail to sway her, but he was desperate, and he couldn't think. A horrible emptiness began to swell inside of him, because he realized that nothing he had said would suffice to turn a daughter away from her own father.

Then she took his hand.

"Mattie . . . " It was all he could say. He was stunned. She knelt beside the bed and laid her head on his shoulder. Putting an arm around her, he held her close. For the first time in his life Addicks felt complete. He'd never realized he *wasn't* whole, until Mattie came along. He felt like shouting out loud with the pure joy of it. Chasing that hideburner and getting shot was the best thing that had ever happened to him.

Outside, Liam was roundly cursing the mules as he tried to put the recalcitrant knobheads in harness. That brought Addicks back down to earth.

"Mattie, bring me my rifle."

She looked into his eyes, concerned, searching for a clue to his intent.

"Don't worry," he said. "I won't hurt him. But there's no telling what he might do when he finds out you're not going with him. He might try to force you to go against your will."

Mattie went to get the Winchester. When she handed the rifle to him he could see that she was still afraid, and he sympathized. Best intentions were one thing, and she believed him when he said he meant her father no harm, but she didn't know how far her father would go.

"*Mattie!*"

She almost jumped out of her skin. It was Liam, calling her.

"Mattie! Get out here. Pronto!"

She looked at Addicks with scared eyes. He put the Winchester under the blanket, against his side, not bothering to check to see if it was loaded. A sensible precaution, under the circumstances, but he was afraid that by doing so he would only add to Mattie's anxiety. The last thing he wanted to do was shoot Liam Henshaw. The idea of killing anybody was abhorrent to him, and filling Mattie's father full of lead right before her eyes would not be a good way to start their lifetime relationship. In this case he was going to have to rely on a bluff.

He took her hand. She was trembling, and he tried to put on a reassuring smile.

"Everything will work out," he said, with counterfeit confidence.

She wasn't fooled. Sitting beside the bed, squeezing her cowboy's hand, Mattie watched the door, knowing that the rest of her life would be shaped by what happened in the next few minutes.

Joaquin Cruz got about a mile from the soddy before sharply checking his roan horse. The *vaquero* cursed softly. He just couldn't do it. He couldn't ride away and let things stand with Addicks. It was true, what they said, about how a person didn't comprehend the full value of something until he had lost it. In this case, the friendship of Addicks Bell was too valuable for Joaquin to let go of it, at least without a fight.

The *vaquero* was somewhat startled to discover that he felt this way about Addicks. He had always made an effort to remain aloof from the rest of the Rimfire outfit. All of the hands respected him, and most liked him personally, but none could honestly claim to be his friend. Not even Shell Harper. That was the way Joaquin liked it. He'd made up his mind a long time back that a man was better off keeping others at arm's length emotionally. Seemed like every time you let yourself care about someone, that person either ended up dead or gone. In fact, one or the other was inevitable. Not so with the land. The land always remained, no matter what. Joaquin felt that it was safe to love the land.

Now, to his amazement, he found he could not turn his back on Addicks. He hadn't thought much of the Illinois farmboy when he first signed on. In fact, he hadn't given Addicks much of a chance at making it as a range rider. But Addicks had surprised everyone with his determination and resilience. He just wouldn't quit. True, he still couldn't shoot worth a damn, but in spite of that shortcoming, Addicks Bell was the kind of man you'd want backing you in a scrape. He would never let you down.

And now Joaquin knew he couldn't let Addicks down.

Addicks' argument was that the land was nowhere near as important as people, and that ran against the grain of everything Joaquin had believed in and lived by since he was old enough to think for himself. The *vaquero* was willing to admit to himself that maybe— just maybe—he'd been wrong on that score.

It occurred to him that Sam Gunnison had thought as he did—that the Rimfire was more important than anything else. More important than family and friendship. Big Sam had been willing to sacrifice everything—his wife, his daughter, even a woman who truly loved him—for the sake of the Rimfire. Joaquin had always admired Big Sam for his single-minded devotion. But maybe Sam had been wrong. It wasn't easy for Joaquin to accept the notion, but there it was. Always he had relied on himself and on the land and never on others. Yet other people *did* matter. *Compadres* like Addicks Bell *did* count for something.

He turned the roan around and rode back the way he had come. Pulled up in the cover of the *brasada* when he saw the wagon in front of the soddy, with the mules in their traces, and wondered what was going on. Dismounting, he sat on his heels, watching and waiting.

21

It didn't take Yantis long to find the place he was looking for. He knew right where to look. The rustler had told him everything he needed to know. With that information the man had purchased his death, and in death a release from pain. That was the way Yantis looked at death, even his own. A release from the never-ceasing agony of life. He felt no remorse in killing people. By killing them he did them a favor. Of course, they never saw it in that light, but Yantis was convinced he was right. Life, as someone had once said, was nasty, brutish, and short. A dreary misery. But there was no misery in the grave. So Yantis didn't mind sending the poor, benighted bastards to a better place, just as he would not mind when it was his time to follow them.

By nightfall he had found it—a soddy on the banks of a rock-strewn creek, nestled against a fifty-foot limestone bluff, half-hidden in a clump of scraggly cottonwoods. A good place for a hideout, a place no one was likely to stumble on. The smoke wisping out of the mudstick chimney was dispersed by a downdraft slipping over the lip of the bluff, so that no one would see it from a distance. The soddy was about as far from any town or road as you could get in this country.

Across the creek from the soddy was a ten-foot

sandy cutbank, and beyond that a brush-covered ridge. Yantis found a vantage point on the ridge and settled down to wait. He counted six horses in the cedar-pole corral, but that didn't tell him how many men were in that soddy. Nightriders generally kept more than one horse handy. Yantis figured two, maybe three men. Six hundred dollars. "How much do you work for, Mr. Yantis?" the Kenton woman had asked. Looking down her long nose at him, like he was not much better than dirt, thinking she was oh so much better than him, and it never occurring to her that she was just as dirty, if not more so. "A hundred dollars," he'd said, paused, smiled, and added, "for each ear." He liked to watch the expressions on their faces when he said that. Surprise, revulsion, and then more superiority, and them not realizing that they were killers just like he was.

Two, maybe three. But he would make sure. He had time, all the time in the world. He never got in a hurry. It wasn't the money. He enjoyed his work. Took pride in a job well done. It was the hunt he relished. The hunt fulfilled him, not the killing. In fact, after the killing was done, he felt empty, unfulfilled all over again. So he savored every moment of the hunt for all it was worth.

In the dying light of sundown he saw a man step out of the soddy. The man looked around, scanning the ridge across the creek. An outlaw was quick to develop the habit of checking the horizon. He looked right at Yantis, but of course did not see him. Yantis was like an Apache. He knew how to blend in. You did not see him until he was in the process of killing you. Finally the man trudged around the corner of the cabin and entered the one-holer. The outhouse was a tilted, rickety structure. When he emerged, Yantis had him in the Big Fifty's leaf sights. Tracked him all the way back into the cabin. His finger lovingly caressed the trigger. But he didn't fire.

A lamp was lighted in the soddy, and the two front windows became square butter-yellow eyes staring back at Yantis through the deepening twilight. Yantis had eyes like a cat's. He could see almost as well in the darkness as he could in full daylight. He saw another man framed for a moment in one of the windows, and even at this distance, almost a hundred yards, Yantis could tell it was not the man who had just visited the outhouse. That made two.

I'll wait until dawn, decided Yantis. At dawn a man usually hadn't had time to put up his guard. And executions were supposed to be at dawn anyway. He watched the cabin for hours, until the lamp was extinguished and the soddy's two square yellow eyes blinked out. Then he lay down on the cold, hard ground, embracing the Sharps, and fell instantly into an untroubled sleep, secure in the knowledge that the faithful buckskin ground-hitched nearby would alert him to an intruder.

As the gray fingers of dawn probed the night's coattails he was up and mounted and riding down to the cutbank, finding a way down that and splashing across the murmuring creek, holding the horse to a walk, with the Big Fifty cradled in his arm. He rode right up to the soddy and just sat there in his saddle and waited.

A wisp of woodsmoke trickled out of the chimney. A little while later the door opened and a man emerged, yawning, scratching at the same time. He was wearing only his longjohns. This was the same man who had visited the outhouse the previous evening. The man pulled up short and gaped when he saw Yantis there, sitting on his horse, the horse and its rider both still as statues.

"Who the hell . . . ?" began the man.

"Yantis is the name," said the regulator, smiling pleasantly. "I ride for the Rimfire."

The man whirled to run back into the soddy, yelling something, but his words of warning stumbled over one another and made no sense. Yantis swung the Big Fifty and fired. The buffalo gun's report was a

shocking intrusion on the morning's tranquility, echo-
ing like a cannon off the limestone bluff. Birds
exploded out of the cottonwoods. The bullet struck
the man squarely between the shoulder blades. His
chest exploded in a spray of rib fragments and blood,
and the impact picked him off his feet and hurled him
through the spray a good ten feet. He hit the hardpack
floor of the soddy as limp and lifeless as a rag doll.

There was only one other man in the soddy. He
commenced to shooting out of one of the windows with
a short gun. But there was nothing to shoot at. Yantis
had vanished. He kept shooting anyway, completely
unnerved, until the gun was empty. He dry-fired several times before that fact penetrated the fog of panic
which enveloped him. It was difficult to reload because
his hands were shaking so. He dropped several "beans."
Then he heard Yantis on the roof, and fired five more
times—he'd forgotten about the sixth chamber in his
haste—up through the sod of the roof. While he was
reloading for the second time, the mudstick chimney
began to regurgitate its smoke, and in a matter of minutes the one room of the soddy was filled with it.

The man cursed and coughed, coughed and
cursed. He was resolved not to be smoked out into the
open, but his resolution was short-lived. Death was
waiting for him outside, but he would die in here if he
stayed. Tears streaming from his burning eyes, he
snatched up a repeater and stumbled out the door.
Turning and firing blindly up at the roof, he worked
the rifle's lever action fast as he could, firing again and
again and again. Then he whirled and ran for the corral.

Yantis appeared out of nowhere, mounted again, to
block his way. The man collided with the horse and fell
down, lost his grip on the rifle. Babbling now, he scrambled to his feet and lurched towards the creek. Yantis
watched him run and laughed softly. The rustler was
only wearing a shirt. Yantis waited until he was in the
creek before shooting. The Big Fifty boomed again. He

aimed for the man's buttocks, and hit the mark. Reloading, he rode up to the creek where the man writhed in the crimson shallows, clutching at the bloody mess of his groin. Yantis gazed dispassionately upon his handiwork. Dismounting, he ground-hitched the horse. The buckskin didn't mind the smell of blood and gun-smoke, and Yantis knew it would stand. Shifting the Sharps to his left hand, he drew a Bowie knife from its belt sheath and moved in to claim the ears. The rustler died before Yantis reached him. The regulator sliced off the ears and put them in a pouch dangling by a string from his belt. Then he walked to the soddy, leading the buckskin, and waded into the smoke-filled dwelling. He grabbed the second rustler by the legs and dragged him out into the open. Another pair of ears was stashed in the pouch. The smoke had affected Yantis, and there were tears on his cheeks.

Four hundred dollars. Yantis was disappointed. Add the man he had killed at the Rimfire ranch house and the two the *vaquero* had done for, and that made five in the gang. Yantis had a feeling five was all there were. The Rimfire's rustling problem was a thing of the past. Too bad, thought Yantis. This had been too quick, too easy. He felt empty.

Climbing into the saddle, he rode over to the corral and let the horses go. They galloped down the creek, splashing through the blood-stained shallows, a couple of them crow-hopping like broncs. Debating whether to return to the Rimfire and collect his bounty and move on, or spend another few days prowling the *brasada* in hopes of adding more ears to his pouch, Yantis opted for the latter. He was in no hurry.

So he rode away, leaving the two dead men to the buzzards, which had already, as though by magic, appeared in the sky. Altogether by chance, he steered a course which would bring him before the day was out to the soddy where Addicks Bell lay in the care of the girl named Mattie.

22

"Jesus, Mattie! We've got to get out of here!"

Mattie pretended not to hear her father. Sitting beside the bed where Addicks lay, she dabbed at the cowboy's forehead with a cool wet cloth.

"Are you deaf as well as dumb?" cried Liam Henshaw, beside himself with anxiety. "Didn't you hear what that *vaquero* said? They've hired a damned regulator. We've got to get out of here. The mules are hitched to the wagon. Now come on."

She did not so much as turn her head, gazing instead at Addicks. She had just given him a shave, and now she touched his cheek with her fingers, and he smiled at her, and she smiled back, her eyes bright in the eternal gloom of the old soddy.

"Mattie," said Liam. His voice had altered in pitch. No longer shrill with panic, deeper now and more menacing, filling with anger. "I ain't never laid a hand on you, gal, but by God I will if you don't mind me. You're coming with me and that's all there is to it."

He took a step toward her.

Addicks brought the Winchester repeater out from under the bedcovers. He didn't aim it straight at Liam. Didn't need to. Liam stopped dead in his tracks at sight of the long gun.

"How'd you get that?"

"She gave it to me. While you were out there hitching up the mules."

"Mattie!" groaned Liam. "How could you betray me thataway? After everything I done for you."

She looked at him then, and defiance blazed in those brown eyes.

"What *have* you done for her?" asked Addicks. "Dragged her from one hellhole to another? Staying in one place only as long as it takes your neighbors to find out what a thief you are? If you cared about your daughter, you'd settle down. Put down roots. Try to make an honest living."

Liam was flabbergasted. An hour ago Addicks had been defending him. But now this! That was gratitude!

"You're one to talk," he said. "A cowboy without nothing to his name but a saddle and an old book."

"I have a home. Rimfire."

"Not anymore you don't."

"Well, no, I guess not. But . . . "

"You reckon you could do better by her?" asked Liam. "You're a half-dead saddle bum."

"If she were mine, I'd work my fingers to the bone to give her what she deserves."

"And what might that be?"

"An honest-to-God home she could call her own, for one thing. Has she ever had that?"

"Once," said Liam, and suddenly all the indignation was gone, and there was a stricken expression on his face. "When her ma was alive. I knew from the start I didn't deserve a woman like that. Oh, she'd ride me purty hard now and then, but I allus deserved *that*. Then she died, when Mattie was just a punkin, and I . . . I started hittin' the bottle and, well, one thing led to another. I deserve the kind of life I got. I ain't good for nothin'." He passed a hand over his face, and turned to his daughter. "I'm sorry, Mattie, gal. Truly sorry."

She put her arms around him, laid her head against his chest. Stroking her hair, Liam looked at Addicks. The Rimfire rider was shocked to see tears brimming in the old squatter's bloodshot eyes.

"Will you give me your word you'll take good care of her, cowboy?"

"I . . ."

"You care about her, don't you?"

"Sure I do. But I can't explain . . . "

"I ain't askin' you to explain. I know she cares about you. Seen it from the start, when I found her up there on that hill, after she'd spent the night stickin' by you, and her scared to death of the dark. That's how it happened with me and her ma. Quick as lightning. I would've done anything for that woman. There ain't no explainin' it. It just happens. Loves like a damned Comanch'—hits you when you least expect it."

Liam pushed Mattie gently away. "You stay here with your cowboy, gal. He'll take good care of you. Lot better care of you than I ever did."

As he turned towards the door Addicks said, "Wait a minute . . . "

"Ain't got a minute," said Liam, his voice husky with emotion. "Got to be movin' on."

He stopped in the doorway.

Yantis was sitting his buckskin in front of the soddy. Horse and rider both were still as statues.

"Morning," said Yantis pleasantly. "This your place?"

Somehow Liam knew beyond a shadow of a doubt who this man was. There was no menace in the man's posture or tone of voice, but the eyes, those cold, blue, piercing eyes, were like mirrors in which Liam could see the reflection of his own death. He felt his nape hairs crawl and the blood turn cold in his veins. He heard a voice in his head. *You're going to die!* screamed the voice. *Run! Run or you will surely die!* But he couldn't run. Couldn't move. His feet seemed to be rooted to the ground.

"Yes," he said, but with no conviction, lying more out of habit than of hope, because he knew this man already had the answer to his question.

Yantis smiled. "Then there's been some mistake. This is Rimfire land. The Rimfire extends all the way west to the San Saba Road."

"No," said Liam flatly, suddenly feeling very tired and old and useless.

"Oh yes. I'm quite certain that's so. You see, I made sure I knew the boundaries. That's how I know you're squatting on Rimfire land."

Liam thought, *I forgot to tell her I love her.*

He turned. "*Mattie!*"

Yantis brought the Sharps to his shoulder and fired.

The impact of the bullet picked Liam up and hurled him through the doorway. His corpse struck the roughhewn table in the center of the room, overturning it.

Her mouth open in a silent scream, Mattie broke away from Addicks' grasp and flew to her father's side.

"Mattie!" yelled Addicks, an echo of Liam Henshaw's final anguished cry. He tried to sit up, but the searing pain in his chest squeezed the breath out of him, and the room began to tilt and spin. Fumbling blindly with the Winchester, he gasped, "Mattie, get away from the door . . . "

Yantis appeared in the doorway, darkening the room as he blocked the daylight. He glanced at Mattie, discounting her as a threat, and then saw Addicks and the rifle. The Sharps swung towards the Rimfire rider.

Mattie threw herself at him, knocking the barrel of the buffalo gun aside just as Yantis squeezed the trigger. The Big Fifty's report was deafening in the close confines of the soddy. The bullet blew a hole in the wall above the bed in which Addicks lay. Addicks couldn't shoot back—Mattie was in the line of fire.

She clawed wildly at the regulator's face, drawing blood. The savagery of her attack caught Yantis by surprise. He stumbled backward out the door. Mattie stayed with him. He used the Sharps to knock her down, backed up three more steps as he plucked another round from the bandolier draped across his chest. Dazed, Mattie got to her feet and came at him again. Yantis didn't have time to reload so he back-handed her. The blow sent her sprawling. This time she was too stunned to get right back up. Recovered now from his surprise, Yantis looked her over and chuckled as he loaded the Big Fifty.

"You have nice ears, gal. Worth a hundred dollars each to me."

He planted the barrel of the buffalo gun between her breasts.

She heard the gunshot. But it wasn't the Sharps which had spoken.

Yantis staggered sideways. Another gunshot, and this time she saw the bullet strike, a puff of dust off the regulator's shirt and a fine, scarlet mist of blood as it exited. Yantis dropped the buffalo gun. Then he crumpled, as though all the bones in his body had turned to dust.

Mattie stared at him, gradually becoming aware of a crunching sound—bootheels grinding the sun-blistered hardpack—and looked up to see Joaquin coming towards her, a rifle in one hand, reins in the other as he led his horse.

"You hurt?" he asked.

She shook her head.

He dropped the reins and held out a gloved hand. She took it, and he helped her to her feet.

"You are *muy valiente*," he said. "Very brave."

"Mattie!"

It was Addicks. Having fallen out of the bed and crawled across the floor of the soddy, he was in the doorway now, but he did not have the strength to go farther.

"Mattie! Thank God!"

She ran to him.

Joaquin hooked a booted foot under the regulator's shoulder and flipped him over on his back. Yantis was still alive, but only just. A bloody froth leaked out of the corners of a mouth curled now in a pain-wracked smile.

"You . . . backshot me," whispered Yantis.

"*Sí,*" said Joaquin, his face a stony mask. "You want to know something? It doesn't bother me."

"No more pain," said Yantis, and the life went out of him.

Joaquin picked up the Big Fifty and walked to the soddy, where Mattie was kneeling in the doorway, cradling Addicks' head in her lap. Throwing caution to the wind, Addicks managed to marshal enough strength to raise an arm and run his fingers through her hair and then pull her head down. He kissed her square on the lips. He'd never done anything half so bold in his life, but he was glad he'd done it—and so was Mattie.

"*Amigo,*" said Joaquin, "I see you are feeling better already."

23

Joaquin buried Liam down by the spring. It occurred to him as he shoveled Rimfire dirt over the blanket-wrapped body that Liam was a squatter even in death. Having lived off someone else's land he was now buried in it, too, and Joaquin felt sorry for him. *But maybe,* mused the vaquero, *I should try to have more compassion.* Maybe it could be said that because Liam Henshaw had spilled his blood on this ground he had as legitimate a claim to it as anyone else.

He felt sorry for Mattie, as well. She helped him pile rocks on top of the grave to keep the coyotes from digging her father's body up. Silent tears streaked her dusty cheeks as she worked. Joaquin said a short prayer, crossed himself, and waited until she was ready to return to the soddy. She did not tarry long over the grave, and had composed herself completely by the time they had walked from the grave to the soddy.

They had put Addicks back to bed. He was conscious, but did not look good, in Joaquin's opinion. His recent exertions had reopened the wound, and now it was the *vaquero*'s turn to sit by and watch while Mattie went to work, changing the bandages.

"I'm glad you came back," said Addicks.

"I never went far."

"You saved Mattie's life."

"But I was too late for her father."

"Why *did* you come back?"

"To tell you I was wrong. To tell you they could stay here as long as they wanted. And to say that I want you to keep riding for the brand."

Addicks was astonished. "I'll be."

Joaquin shrugged. "You were right. I don't know how many cattle there are on Rimfire range. So how could we miss one or two?"

"But will Emmy Gunnison feel the same way?"

Again Joaquin shrugged.

"It doesn't matter," said Addicks. "Liam's dead." He shook his head. "I can't stay on, Joaquin."

"Why not?"

Addicks looked at Mattie. "I've got somebody else to think of now."

"She is welcome at the ranch."

"No. We need a place of our own. She sure does. It's something she's never had."

"But what will you do?"

"I could always go back to farming."

"A sodbuster!" Joaquin was shocked.

Addicks laughed, then winced, because it hurt to laugh. "I've never met a cattleman who wasn't prejudiced against farmers. Farmers aren't so bad, Joaquin, once you get to know them."

"It isn't the farmer. It's what he does to the land. You came to Texas to become a cowboy, to get away from that life."

"That's gospel truth. I did. Reckon I would prefer to run cattle, but that takes money, and I'm afraid I haven't got much of a grubstake."

"I have an idea." Joaquin rose from the bench he's been sitting on, walked the length of the soddy and back, then sat down again. "Why don't you take this land? From here west to the San Saba Road, and north to Dog Creek. And all the mavericks that are on it."

Addicks couldn't believe his ears. "Lord, Joaquin. That's . . . it's a good five miles to the road from here. Must be . . . I don't know . . . hundreds of unbranded cattle on the land you're talking about."

"*Sí.* At least."

"If this is one of your jokes . . . "

"No joking."

"I couldn't," said Addicks. "I won't accept charity."

"Then you can pay for it."

"I told you, I'm flat busted."

"We'll take payment in cattle. Every other calf that is born on this land we will take."

"Every maverick, and every calf that's born on this land belongs to the Rimfire. You can't speak for Emmy Gunnison. She'd never go for that deal."

"Yes, she would. If it is what I want to do, she will do it."

Addicks peered at him with narrowed eyes. "There's something you're not telling me, Joaquin. Or else you've been chewing locoweed. One or the other."

Joaquin took a deep breath. "What I am about to tell you no one else but Emmy knows. Maria Arista was my mother."

He paused, watching Addicks intently to see what his reaction would be, and he did not have to say anything more.

Maria Arista was my mother. Five words that spoke volumes. Addicks Bell had spent his childhood working his father's wheat fields, and his schooling had been sporadic, to say the least. He was a completely self-educated man. His mind was quick, and he could figure out the rest of the story on his own.

"You're saying Sam Gunnison was your father."

Joaquin nodded. "When my mother went to him and said she was carrying his child, they both agreed it would be better if she went away. She had worked several years as his housekeeper. Keeping house was something his wife knew nothing about, and had no desire to learn. Sam Gunnison was no longer in love with his wife, but she had borne him a son, and was pregnant with Emmy at the time, and though he had strong feelings for my mother, he would not risk losing his family. He knew his wife would leave the Rimfire, and take the children with her, and he could not bear for that to happen.

"My mother was living in San Saba when I was born. Sam Gunnison made certain that she had food and shelter and a doctor's care on the occasion of my birth. He never came to see her, and everything he gave, which is more than most men would have given in his place, he gave through a friend of his who lived in San Saba, and who could be relied on to act discreetly.

"But Sam Gunnison could not bear to remain apart from my mother, and soon after I was born he asked her to come back to the Rimfire. Only she could not bring me with her. You see, *Señora* Gunnison had long suspected that there was something between her husband and my mother. He was afraid that if my mother came back with me, his wife would know the truth. At first my mother refused to leave me, but then, finally, she changed her mind. I was left in San Saba, in the keeping of a good woman who had befriended my mother. My mother knew I would be well cared for, and I was.

"I know what you are thinking, *amigo*. How could a mother leave her infant son? She did it for my sake. She was determined, somehow, to see that I received my rightful inheritance. When I was a young boy, she would sometimes take me aside and tell me how my father was a great and powerful man, and that some-day I would have what was rightfully mine."

"So what happened?" asked Addicks. "Why didn't Sam Gunnison ever admit he was your father?"

Joaquin smiled faintly. "My mother died when I was fourteen. Standing over her grave, Sam Gunnison asked me to come to work for him. By that time his wife had left him anyway. His son was dead. I joined the Rimfire outfit. He would admit to me that he was my father, but to no one else. And he never asked me not to tell anyone what I knew. But I never did."

"Why not?"

"Pride. I was too proud. I know that may not make much sense to you, but I think that is why I kept the secret. And I never asked him to speak of it."

"I'm surprised you didn't hate his guts."

"So am I. But I could not. I don't know why he never told anyone. I think maybe it was pride in his case, too. I don't know. I'm not certain about that part of it."

"You said Emmy knows?"

"Yes. He did tell her one day. There was a big fight. She wanted him to acknowledge me before the whole world. He refused, and she went away."

"So she's your half-sister."

"*Sí.* That is how I know she will do what I want about this land."

"That makes half the Rimfire yours."

"It is true, Emmy would share it with me. She will probably insist on it. But I will say no if she does. I do not want to live in the big house. I like my life the way it is. The Rimfire is my home. That's all I need to know. No one else needs to know more. And no one can take it away from me. This is why I want your word that you will tell no one else what you have heard today. I will make Emmy promise me the same thing."

"If that's what you want . . . "

"It is."

"Then you have my word."

"*Bueno.*" Joaquin stood up. "Then you will accept my offer?"

Addicks glanced at Mattie, unsure. Her eyes said it all—the decision was his. She would stay here with him, or go wherever he wanted to go.

"I won't take so much," he said. "A man needs to start out small and build his future. It isn't good to have everything handed to you on a silver platter. There's no sense of accomplishment that way. You appreciate what you work for, not what's given you. And what I do take I'll pay for, in the manner you've described. Every other calf will wear a Rimfire brand."

Joaquin extended a hand. Addicks took it.

And so the deal was done, a contract made, as surely as if it were etched in stone.

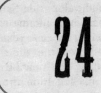

With each passing mile Shell Harper became ever more convinced that he and Emmy ought to turn back. Going after Billy Bishop and his gang of hellions was sheer suicide. There were seven of them—the tracks were plain enough. Seven against two. Those were a fool's odds. True, Emmy was an accomplished shot, and no one acquainted with her could doubt for a moment that she had the courage of ten ordinary men. She was carrying O'Hara's scattergun, with about a dozen extra shells, and Jack Ember's revolver. The revolver and the shells were rolled up in the apron taken from the stage station and tied around her trim waist. With those weapons she could do a lot of damage. But had she ever killed a man? If so, it had to have happened in St. Louis, and Shell thought that was highly unlikely, given what he knew about her high society life there. He knew she was capable of doing it—but would she hesitate? Hesitation could prove fatal against such men. They killed without compunction or remorse. Their own lives meant precious little to them—life on the dodge was not something to be cherished—and cared even less for the lives of others.

Shell could vividly remember the one and only

time he had been forced to kill a man. Every detail was burned indelibly into his memory. In his nineteenth year he had fought alongside Sam Gunnison in a range war which had become infamous in the violent panorama of Texas frontier lore as a result of its particularly vicious nature. When the time came he had frozen, for just an instant, and now he would forever carry an ugly scar on his leg from the man's bullet. He'd been lucky that hesitation had not cost him his life, and he was sure he would not hesitate again under similar circumstances.

Still, the odds were too high, and it only made matters excruciatingly worse that he was in love with Emmy. To think of her in mortal danger was unbearable. Yet what could he do, short of physically restraining her? He could hogtie her and drag her screaming and kicking all the way back to the Rimfire. That way, at least, she would still be alive. He gave that idea a whole lot of thought all morning as they followed the trail, and might have gone through with it, had the situation not changed so drastically and in such an unexpected manner.

Though unaccustomed to riders, the horses did not give them any more trouble than they could handle. Deft knife work on Shell's part with some rope and the leather from the stage company harness had produced two makeshift "ear head" bridles. He could not fail to notice how well Emmy rode, even bareback. Horses and riding had always been her passion, as he recalled.

A few miles from the stage station at Hollering Woman Creek, the seven desperadoes had stopped and waited out the night. Theirs had been a cold camp, deep in a mesquite thicket. No fire, no food, no coffee, and by the looks of things not much sleeping, either. Shell and Emmy found the butts of numerous spent cigarettes and an empty bottle of rotgut whiskey. Shell wondered that Bishop hadn't thought to abscond with the bottles of fine Kentucky bourbon which had served so well as an integral part of Mr. Teague's convincing disguise. Clearly an oversight on his part.

Shell could picture them in his mind's eye: seven furtive men, sitting in the darkness, watching and listening to the night and its sounds, holding their horses ready for a quick getaway, smoking and drinking to smooth the wrinkles out of their nerves. Knowing that several people had survived the ambush at the stage station, Bishop had to be wondering how long it would take for word to spread. When it did, the whole state would be swarming with lawmen and bounty hunters. Shell wondered what kind of price Bishop had on his head. Whatever the current amount, it would skyrocket now. Two men had been gunned down, and worst of all for Bishop and his gang, one of those was a Texas Ranger. That meant every Ranger in the state would be after them with a vengeance. The Rangers did not take lightly the killing of one of their own. Ember's death would not go unavenged.

The seven outlaws had waited for first light to proceed, and Shell surmised that they had done so to avoid blundering into trouble in the darkness. Their pause closed the gap between pursuer and pursued— Shell calculated that the desperadoes were now only a few hours ahead of them. Bishop wasn't making haste. He was leading his men carefully cross-country, avoiding the roads and the occasional farm and hamlet. Always heading north by northwest. Shell wondered if they were making for the Indian Nations, that notorious haven for the lawless.

Then, in the early afternoon, he and Emmy found the bloodstains.

The sign here was confused, but there was no question that someone had been shot. There was no indication that the gang had run afoul of the law or an honest citizen—in fact, there was no sign of anyone but the seven longriders, and no sign of a fight, either. Shell puzzled over this for a spell.

"I don't know, Emmy," he said, finally. "What do you think?"

"I think they had a falling out," she replied, having examined the sign herself and reached her own conclusions. "I think one of them killed another."

"If so, you'd expect to find the body. They wouldn't waste time burying him. And why would they take him along?"

An answer came to him even as he asked the question, and a glance at Emmy told him that she was thinking along the same lines.

"The bounty," she said.

He nodded. "Sure. The bounty. A couple of things that Ranger said are coming back to me now."

"Such as?"

"For one thing, that the law didn't know the identities of several of the men who rode with Bishop. He was counting on Bishop spilling the beans about those men, and where they were holed up."

"Men like Teague."

"Yeah. And then he said he figured the gang would try to free Bishop. Not to save his bacon so much as to save their own, because they knew Bishop would talk if they let him go to the gallows."

Emmy nodded. "I think I know what you're getting at."

"I'll bet you it was Billy Bishop who got killed here."

"And one of those men the law doesn't know will turn his body in for the reward. It's dead or alive. There's no honor among thieves, they say."

"Maybe Teague."

"One way to find out," said Emmy, and mounted up.

Following the trail, they arrived at a road an hour prior to sunset. Here the outlaws had split up. Four of them rode north, deeper into rough country, while two proceeded to the northwest on the road.

"If we're right," said Shell, "that would be the one who's taking the dead man in for the reward. I don't know this country, but I have a hunch there'll be a town not too far up this road."

They pressed on, and arrived at the small community of China Spring less than an hour later. There wasn't much to the town. Shell guessed that maybe two hundred people, all told, resided here. And when they reached the main thoroughfare, a wide, rutted hardpack lined with false-front clapboards sprinkled with a few more substantial brick structures, they came upon such a crowd that Shell decided the entire population was congregated. The Rimfire foreman cornered a man who was quartering across the street, his long strides and excited air testifying to the fact that he was in a big hurry to get somewhere.

"What's going on?" asked Shell.

"That's what I'm trying to find out myself," said the man, annoyed by this delay. "I hear tell somebody brought in an outlaw with his toes curled. They say it might be Billy Bishop. But I dunno about that. If you'd move that cayuse out of my path I could get on up to the jailhouse and find out. You can't believe anything you don't see with your own two eyes. So if you don't mind . . ."

"Much obliged." Shell moved his horse and let the man pass.

The focus of the crowd's attention seemed to be a clapboard building halfway along the street, and the crowd was so dense that Emmy and Shell could get no closer than fifty yards. Shell dismounted and handed the makeshift reins to Emmy.

"Wait here. I'll go find out."

He plunged into the crowd, shouldering his way through the press, ignoring the indignant curses of the men he jostled as he made his way to the clapboard building, which he assumed was the local jail and office of the town sheriff. It was rough going, and took a while, but he persevered, and reached the boardwalk fronting the building. Here he found two men holding back the eager onlookers with their stern expressions and sawed-off shotguns. When someone seemed about to climb up onto the boardwalk, a sharp look and a slight movement of the scatterguns were sufficient to dissuade them.

Between the two guards lay a body. A blanket covered it completely, which aggravated the crowd to no end. A dozen voices hurled questions at the guards. "Who is it?" "Is that Billy Bishop?" "Who killed him?" "Where's the sheriff, we want to know." But the guards ignored these queries. Shell could sympathize with the crowd. He could scarcely refrain from leaping onto the boardwalk and ripping the blanket away. But he didn't, and concentrated on keeping his place in the front row of the unruly crowd, no mean feat.

A few minutes later a burly man with craggy features and a badge on his coat stepped out of the jail-house, carrying a lantern in one hand and a repeating rifle in the other. When they saw him the crowd of townsfolk got louder, and the jostling more pronounced. Now it seemed as though everyone was firing a question, and the clamor made Shell wince. The sheriff scanned the crowd with mild disgust. Putting down the lantern, he swung the rifle up and fired a round through the roof of the boardwalk. The crowd fell silent and grew quite still.

"That's better," said the sheriff. "Now what's all this ruckus about? I want one man to answer."

"We want to know who the dead man is, Sheriff," said someone behind Shell.

The sheriff nodded. "A reasonable request." He bent down and flipped the blanket aside. The crowd began to move again, surging forward, everyone straining to see. The China Spring badgetoter tossed his rifle to one of his shotgun-toting deputies and then reached down to lift the corpse, holding it in front of him, his arms locked around the dead man's chest.

It was Billy Bishop.

Shell had an advantage over the people in the crowd. Nary a one of them had seen Bishop in the flesh, though most had seen an artist's rendition on a wanted poster, or read a newspaper description.

"Is that him?" someone asked. "Is that Billy Bishop?"

"Yes," said the sheriff.

"Who's the feller who brought him in?"

"What business is that of yours, Frank?"

"Where was Bishop shot, Sheriff? I heard he was shot in the back."

"As a matter of fact, he was. In my book, that's a good place to shoot a man like this. Would any of you have done different? I doubt it. Bishop didn't deserve better."

With that the sheriff let the body go. It hit the boardwalk with a heavy thump. The sheriff picked up the blanket and dropped it negligently on the corpse, covering the head and torso.

"Now," he said, "I want you folks to get on home."

For a moment no one moved.

The sheriff glanced at the deputy who held his rifle. The deputy tossed the rifle back to him.

"Git," said the sheriff. "Don't make me say it again."

The crowd dispersed, a few of them mumbling complaints about the rough handling they were receiving from the man with the badge. But none of them complained too loudly.

Shell made his way back to Emmy, who was still sitting her horse in the middle of the street.

"It's Bishop," he said. "We were right."

"Who brought him in?"

"I don't know. Does it matter? Bishop's dead, Emmy. Let's go home."

"Not a chance," she said sharply.

"Emmy . . . "

"That man Teague killed a Texas Ranger, Shell. And I have a feeling it was Teague who brought Bishop in."

"Fine," sighed Shell. "Let's go tell the sheriff what happened. *Then* we can go home."

"We can't do that."

"Why the h . . . I mean, why-in-the-abiding-place-of-the-unregenerate-sinful not?"

"Because Teague might be in there with the sheriff right now. If we capture Teague now, the rest of the gang will get away. They must be waiting somewhere outside of town. Waiting to split the reward for Bishop. Teague—or whoever brought Bishop in—can lead us right to them."

"Not us." Shell shook his head. "The sheriff and his deputies. But not us. They look like they can handle the job."

"I'm not going home until Teague at least gets his comeuppance."

"Emmy, please be reasonable . . . "

Emmy looked at a building up the street to the left, across from the jailhouse. "There's a hotel. We'll stay there tonight."

"I haven't got two dollars to rub together."

"I've got money enough for a room."

"*A* room?"

Her smile was a bit mischievous, he thought. "I mean *two* rooms, of course."

Shell threw up his hands. "Okay," he said, exasperated. "I could use a bath and a hot meal."

They tied their horses to the hitching post in front of the hotel and went inside.

At that moment a bearded man wearing a gray longcoat and riding a gray horse rode into China Spring from the south.

25

Shell found out from the clerk working the hotel desk that the best place in China Springs to eat was at Miss Laidlaw's down at the north end of the street. Apparently, Miss Laidlaw had been a Harvey girl in her younger days. Rumor had it that a traveling man broke her heart, and she'd vowed never to trust another man. So far she had kept faith with herself, though she was a handsome woman, said the clerk in a wistful way, and many were the bachelors who courted her, so far to no avail. She made money as a seamstress and a tutor and opened her dining room to the public. A young Mexican woman helped her in the kitchen.

Having been subjected to the history of Miss Laidlaw as the price for information on where to find victuals, Shell had second thoughts about asking the talkative clerk about baths, but he figured he ought to wash some of the dust and grime off if he was going to sit down to table in a spinster lady's home. The Chinaman next door, said the clerk, had a room in back of his laundry where a feller could partake of a nice, hot bath for four bits, and could even douse his bath water with smell pretty for an extra two bits, were he so inclined.

Shell thought that was a little high for a bath, and said so. The clerk agreed, but ever since by town ordinance the locals had made the nearby spring and creek off limits to bathers, as that was one of the town's primary sources of drinking water, the Chinaman had cornered the public bath market and knew it. He was right high with his charges for laundering services, too, in the clerk's opinion, but then wasn't that just like a heathen Chinee? It was rumored that the Chinaman had once operated an opium den, somewhere in California, and the citizens of China Springs were keeping a close eye on him, as he was pretty thoroughly disliked by just about everyone.

They got adjacent rooms on the second floor of the hotel. The clerk wanted to know everything about them. Where they came from, where they were going, why they were here in China Springs, how come they didn't have any personal belongings aside from a rifle and a revolver and a scattergun—the clerk couldn't see the other revolver, rolled up in Emmy's apron—and why there were riding cayuses which were obviously not saddle horses. Shell and Emmy knew better than to tell him much of anything, for it was evident that whatever they said in response to this interrogation would circulate through town quick as a grassfire . . .

"We've come to see the sheriff," said Emmy, with a sweet smile, and left it at that. The clerk's curiosity was piqued by this cryptic answer, but he could get nothing more out of them.

"Now at least you won't have to sit outside my door," said Emmy, as they reached their rooms. "If I want you I'll just pound on the wall."

Shell's room had one window, with a scenic view of the alley between the hotel and the Chinaman's laundry. He left the room and knocked on Emmy's door. She called to him to enter.

"Emmy, I wish you'd lock this door when . . . "

She was standing at her window, and motioned for him to come closer. From the window he could look directly across the street at the jailhouse.

The sheriff and Teague had just emerged. Standing over the corpse of Billy Bishop, they talked for a moment. Then Teague nodded and started across the street, making for the hotel.

"Get back," said Shell. "He might look up and see us."

There were no curtains on the window, and Shell realized they were framed against the amber glow of the lamp Emmy had lighted. But Teague didn't look up. The sheriff spoke to the deputies and went back inside the jailhouse. The deputies put down their scatterguns and carried Bishop's body up the street. Shell moved to the door, put his ear to it, and listened. A moment later he heard footsteps in the hallway. A door opened and closed. The Rimfire foreman opened the door slightly, and saw a strip of lamplight beneath the door to the room across the hall.

Rejoining Emmy at the window, he said, "That man's got a lot of nerve."

"I'm going to talk to the sheriff."

"Good. Then we can go home."

"Not yet. When they capture Bishop's gang I want to be there."

"Why do you have to be so all-fired stubborn, Emmy?"

"Runs in the family."

"It must. But I'd like to see you talk that tin star into letting you ride with the posse."

"I'll ride with it or without it, but I'll be there."

Shell just shook his head.

"You go have your bath," said Emmy. "Leave the sheriff to me."

"I'm sticking with you," he sighed.

"Oh, for heaven's sake. Are you still worried about Buckhorn's hired gun?"

"I am, and you should be too."

O'Hara's shotgun lay on the bed. Emmy picked it up.

"I am perfectly capable of taking care of myself," she told him. "I believe I can get safely across the street with this, thanks all the same."

Shell grimaced. "You're too hard-headed for your own good. Have it your own way."

"Are you sure that's why you're sticking to me, Shell?" she asked coquettishly. "I thought maybe it was because you liked me."

Flustered, he went downstairs with her. They parted company in front of the hotel, she crossing the street to the jailhouse and he ambling down to the Chinaman's place, lingering at the door to that establishment until Emmy was safely inside the sheriff's office.

He spent twenty minutes soaking his aching body in the iron clawfoot tub filled to the brim with water, a rare luxury for a cowboy. He figured he'd earned it, having ridden over hundreds of miles of rough country and even been shot at. The depressing part about it was that he still wasn't any closer to getting Emmy Gunnison home to the Rimfire than he'd been from the get-go. But, as frustrating as it all was, he had to admire her courage.

And he wondered if she was right—was he using Pratt as an excuse to stick as close to her as her own shadow? In truth, he was beginning to wonder about Pratt. Maybe the man wasn't going to show after all. Surely he would have made his move by now. And if he was looking for Emmy on the stageline, the last place he'd pop up was China Springs.

For the first time in a coon's age he was beginning to relax. A pleasant feeling—but short-lived, because Emmy came through the curtained door without a by-your-leave.

"Emmy!" he yelped. "Have you got no shame?"

He scrunched down in the clawfoot tub and thanked the Lord that the water was muddied up with about ten pounds of Texas dirt.

She laughed. "My goodness, Shell. If we're going to be married, you'll have to get over being so modest sooner or later."

"Married?"

"You *are* going to marry me, aren't you?"

"Well, I . . . uh, I . . . "

"I thought so. I've always thought we'd be married someday."

Shell was speechless.

"You'll get around to asking, eventually," she said. "But don't worry about that now." She spotted a three-legged stool in a corner; carrying it over to the tub, she sat down with the shotgun across her knees and leaned forward. "I talked to the sheriff. Told him what happened. All about Teague."

"What did he say?"

"Oh, he believed me. I knew he would. Father's name counts for something, even way up here. He agreed that the best thing to do would be to let Teague lead us to the rest of the gang. The sheriff had sent a telegram to Austin confirming that Bishop's been brought in. Once it has the state's promise to reimburse, the bank here will pay the reward. By noon tomorrow Teague should have the bounty and be on his way."

"What did Teague tell the sheriff?"

"That he was passing through, heading for San Antone to find work. Said Bishop rode into his camp last night, had a cup of his coffee, and then tried to rob him. But he got careless, didn't think Teague had a gun, and Teague shot him down. The sheriff said he thought the story sounded fishy to him."

"It's on account of how Teague looks."

"That's right. No one would take him for a cold-blooded killer. That's what makes him so dangerous."

"You said 'us.'"

"What?"

"You said, 'Let Teague lead *us* to the rest of the gang.'"

"Well, the sheriff didn't exactly cotton to the idea of our going along. But I told him we were going anyway, with or without him."

"And what did he say to that?"

"He said he'd throw us in jail if we tried," she said, in a deliberately offhand manner.

"Stop being so mule-headed, Emmy. Tomorrow morning we're going home."

"Maybe you are. I'm not."

"Yes, you are."

"No, I'm not." She stood up, her eyes flashing defiance. "I don't like being told what to do."

"You're as spoiled and willful as ever."

"Don't forget you work for me now, Shell Harper. You'll do what I say or I'll hogleg you off the Rimfire payroll."

That riled him. "By gum I think you would, too."

"Try me." She turned on her heel and marched out of the room.

"I'm getting mighty tired of following you all over Texas!" he yelled after her.

But she was gone.

Perturbed, he sat there in his fast-cooling bath and fumed. He couldn't believe Emmy had threatened to fire him—and that not minutes after talking about marriage! It made absolutely no sense to him why she was so adamant about pursuing the outlaw gang to the bitter end. What was she trying to prove? That she was Sam Gunnison's daughter? That she had the *cajones* to run the Rimfire, even if she *was* a woman? Or maybe she really did honestly believe that it was every citizen's responsibility to fight the lawless element tooth and nail and hang the cost.

Whatever her true motives, Shell concluded that it really didn't matter as far as he was concerned. His anger quickly ebbed. Tired or not, he would follow her to hell and back again. Stepping out of the bath, he dressed hurriedly, paid the Chinaman his four bits, and left the laundry.

As he crossed the mouth of the alley between the laundry and the hotel he heard the soft whicker of a horse, and looked down the alley to see the animal tied up at the other end, at the back corner of the hotel. Something told him he ought to get a closer look at that whey-belly, and he bent his steps in that direction.

He was halfway down the alley when, his vision having adjusted to the night, he recognized the horse.

It was the dappled gray he'd seen in front of the Bull's Eye Saloon in Lampasas, the day Buckhorn and Pratt met there.

Pratt's horse.

Buckhorn's hired gun was in China Springs!

26

He was waiting for her in the room, standing with his back to the wall, behind the door when it opened, and she knew something was wrong as soon as she stepped across the threshold, but it was too late. As he grabbed her he kicked the door shut. Emmy's first thought was of Shell. Not wishing he was here so much as wishing she had listened to his advice about locking her door. She had never taken him seriously about Buckhorn's hired gun.

Emmy tried to bring O'Hara's scattergun to bear, and wasted precious seconds in the futile attempt—futile because he was too strong, and had one big, gloved hand clasped over the double barrel. Belatedly she thought if I can just shoot, even if I don't hit him, a shotgun blast ought to bring somebody. Before she could do it, though, Pratt was twisting the weapon out of her hand. As she fought him the apron around her waist came undone, and the extra shells and the Ranger's gun fell onto the floor.

Once he had the weapon, he gave her a hard shove. She caught herself on the corner of the bed, turned to face him, and saw that the shotgun was turned on her now.

"Scream, and I'll blow a hole through you."

She hadn't even considered screaming. That wasn't her style.

"I heard that Buckhorn doesn't want me dead," she said.

He leered at her through his black beard. "Oh, he does. He just doesn't have the guts to pay for murder. I'm the one who don't want you dead. But then, we don't always get what we want."

Emmy knew better than to panic. Panic never helped anything. In a tight spot you had to remain calm, and keep thinking—it was your only hope.

"I ought to be flattered," she said. "You've come a long way just to meet me."

She had him thinking now. His brow was slightly furrowed. "You talk like you were expecting me."

"We know all about you and your deal with Buckhorn. So you might as well forget it and ride on."

"Oh, I thought about doing that. Thought about it long and hard. But then I figured, what the hell, I ought to see what she looks like, anyhow. And when I saw you, I decided it was worth the risk. So you're coming with me, little lady. We'll have a high ol' time, you and me."

"I'm not going anywhere with you."

Pratt chuckled. He kicked the revolver into a corner of the room and stepped towards her. "You can fight it, or you can just settle back and enjoy it. Don't matter. You're going to get it, either way."

The door seemed to disintegrate in an explosion of splintered wood, cracking back against the wall. Pratt whirled and triggered one barrel of the scattergun. The weapon's roar was deafening in the close confines of the room. But the double-ought missed Shell completely and shredded what was left of the door, hanging now by one hinge. The Rimfire foreman had hit the door with such force that when it gave way he pitched forward, losing his balance, and the buckshot sailed over his head. He plowed into Pratt, tackling him around the knees. But Pratt refused to go down. He struck with the shotgun, and the double barrel hammered Shell across the shoulder. A blast of searing pain made him loosen his grasp on Pratt, and he tried to roll away, out of Pratt's reach, knowing that Pratt was trying to split his skull open and not wanting to give him a second chance. As he rolled he tried to fish the Remington Army out of its holster, but he was slow, too slow, and he saw Pratt level the shotgun at him.

Emmy threw herself forward, not at Pratt, but at the shotgun, and they wrestled for the weapon, and Pratt hit her with his fist, squarely on the jaw. Emmy slumped, dazed. But she wouldn't relinquish her hold on the shotgun.

"Emmy!" cried Shell, because Pratt could trigger that other barrel of double-ought, and if he did it would cut her in two.

But Pratt didn't fire. He'd come all this way, not to kill Emmy Gunnison, but to have her, and he hadn't given up on that notion just yet. So he pushed her roughly away and let her take the scattergun with her. Whipping the longcoat aside he drew his six-shooter. Up on one knee, Shell was drawing the Remington. They fired almost simultaneously. Shell didn't even feel the bullet graze his ribcage. Pratt doubled over, clutching at his belly. He staggered, fetched up against the window, slowly brought the gun to bear on Shell, and then caught just a glimpse of Emmy, rising from the floor and, as she did so, bringing the shotgun to chest-level. The last thing he saw was the blossom of flame from the scattergun's barrel through wreaths of gray gunsmoke.

The impact of a full load of double-ought punched him through the window. His corpse hit the boardwalk roof and fell through to land on the weathered planks below.

Emmy threw the empty shotgun down and went to Shell.

"You're wounded," she said.

"Just a scratch." He touched her cheek, where a bruise was already showing. "The bastard hit you."

"It doesn't hurt."

"You're a hell of a woman, Emmy Gunnison."

Then he remembered Teague—and rushed out of the room.

"Shell?"

He knocked down his second door of the evening, swept an empty room with the Remington, and saw the open window.

Emmy was standing in the hallway.

"Teague's gone," he said.

"I'm not surprised."

He felt the pain then, and winced, and she took his arm and led him back into her room. Sat him on the bed and began to unbutton his blood-soaked shirt.

"I'm modest," he said. "Remember?"

"You'll get over it."

He gazed up into the most beautiful blue eyes he had ever seen.

"Emmy, will you marry me?"

"Of course," she said, in that offhand way he found so infuriating.

"I mean it."

"I know you mean it. As long as you remember that I'm the boss."

He laughed. "Oh, no."

"Oh, yes. You'll see."

The China Springs sheriff's brawny form filled the doorway. He looked at them, somewhat askance, and walked over to the shattered window, leaning out to look down through the ragged hole in the board-walk roof at Pratt.

"That feller's defunct," he observed. "Killed several times over. You all want to tell me why?"

"It's a long story," said Shell.

The sheriff grimaced. A crowd was gathering in

the street below. "Those people. You'd think they had nothing better to do than stare at dead bodies." He turned back into the room. "I like stories."

"Teague's gone," said Emmy. "Must have bolted when the shooting started."

"Figured as much."

"Aren't you going after him?"

"Me? What about you, Miss Gunnison?"

Emmy looked at Shell and smiled. "No. I'm going home—with my future husband."

"Huh." The sheriff looked Shell over and didn't appear too impressed by Emmy's taste. He walked to the door, and paused.

"Don't reckon I'll need to chase him all over Texas, ma'am. I'll just make certain there's a nice, big reward put on his scalp. After all, he killed a Texas Ranger. I'll wager one of them boys in the gang will get a bright idea about collecting that bounty. What do you think?"

"I like it," said Emmy.

"You all come see me before you leave town," said the sheriff.

He touched the brim of his hat and walked out.

"Should've asked him about a doctor," said Shell, grimacing at the pain.

"You don't need a doctor. You've got me."

EPILOGUE

In his office with his feet propped up on his desk, Moss Buckhorn gazed at the framed map of Lampasas and the surrounding country which hung in a prominent place on the wall. His ranch, to the west of town, was outlined in red, and he tried to imagine how it would look with the Rimfire, clearly delineated on the map, outlined in the same manner.

Soon it would be his. He was sure of that. Emmy Gunnison was long overdue, and no word. He could only assume that Pratt had done his job. *In a week or two*, mused Buckhorn, *I will ride out there, commiserate with Mrs. Kenton, and then make my offer. She will refuse it, at first. Hope springs eternal, after all. But as the weeks stretch into months, and Emmy is still missing, she will reconsider.*

Yes, the Rimfire would belong to him. He poured himself another shot of Old Overshoe, and toasted the map. Someday he would own it all, and he would be the biggest man in Texas. Maybe he'd even run for governor someday. His prospects were as boundless as his ambition.

Maybe someday I will marry, he thought. *Problem is, you're supposed to share your life with your spouse, and I don't want to share anything. I'm the one who has worked to get everything I have now, and I'll be damned if I'll . . .*

He heard the door of the front office open, listened, expecting to hear the voice of Mr. Ledbetter, his clerk. But he heard only the clump of bootheels, and premonition of disaster caused him to swing his feet down off the desk and open the top right drawer. That was where he kept his pistol, a Porterhouse .38.

The door swung open, and Shell Harper stepped in. Buckhorn thought the barrel of the Remington Army Model in the Rimfire foreman's hand looked as big as a cannon's.

"What's the meaning of this, Harper?" growled Buckhorn. "Who do you think you are, barging in here like this? What have you done to Mr. Ledbetter?"

"He's taking a long walk. If you have a gun in that drawer, I sure wish you'd go for it."

Buckhorn smiled and slowly shut the drawer, laid his hands flat on top of the desk.

"You've never liked me, Harper. I've often wondered why. I've never done anything to you."

"It's not what you've done so much as what you are that bothers me."

"And what am I?" sneered Buckhorn.

"I'd like to tell you, but there's a lady present." Shell stepped aside and said, "Emmy."

The color drained from Buckhorn's face as Emmy Gunnison walked in.

"Hello, Mr. Buckhorn."

He swallowed hard and just stared at all his dreams of glory turned to ashes.

"I wanted you to see that I'm home," she said. "Since you're a friend of the family, I knew you'd be happy to know that."

Buckhorn was quick to recover. He stood up and came around the desk, scornfully ignoring Shell and the Remington, and extending his hand to Emmy.

"It's so good to see you again, Emmy, after all these years."

"Is it? I bet you're surprised."

"I was worried about you. You were overdue."

"Is that why you sent that man Pratt to find me?"

"I don't know what you're talking about. I know no one by that name."

"You're a slick liar," said Shell.

"I don't have to take that from the likes of you."

"I say we just shoot daylight through him, Emmy."

"You'd hang," said Buckhorn.

"It would be worth it to rid the world of your shadow."

"No," said Emmy. "He's not worth killing."

She hit him.

Buckhorn was completely off guard. It was the last thing he expected Emmy to do. Her fist slammed into his smirking mouth and knocked him backward. He fetched up against the desk, with the copper taste of blood in his mouth, and hot anger blazing in his eyes.

"You bitch . . ."

Shell punched him then, and he fell to his hands and knees, drooling blood. The Rimfire foreman holstered the Remington and hauled Buckhorn to his feet and slammed him against the wall, hard enough to shake the entire land office.

"Where are your manners?" rasped Shell. "That's no way to talk to a lady."

"Go to . . ."

Shell drove a fist into his belly. Buckhorn jack-knifed and pitched forward, and Shell let him fall.

"It's not over," wheezed Buckhorn. "It's not over."

"He's almost as stubborn as you are, Emmy," observed Shell. He felt good, having wanted to deliver that punch for a good many years now.

"You'll never have the Rimfire, Mr. Buckhorn," Emmy said. "It's not just land and cattle, and it doesn't just belong to me. It's a home and a promise to a lot of others, and I'll never let you get your hands on it."

"You're not Sam Gunnison. You can't hold onto it."

"Watch me," she said, and looked at Shell, and smiled. "I have a lot of good help."

Joaquin Cruz was waiting for them outside in the street. They rode together, the three of them, out of Lampasas, across the shallows of the ford at the river, and along the road, then up the rock-strewn slope of the long ridge to the graves beneath the tall Rimfire oaks. Emmy and Joaquin dismounted. She stood pensively at the foot of her father's grave, while the *vaquero* knelt and prayed, head bowed, at his mother's final resting place.

Shell sat his saddle astride the lanky sorrel gelding he called Lucifer, recently arrived from Spanish Station, courtesy of the Widow Stanton, and good as new. The Rimfire foreman plumbed the depths of his innermost feelings. He could accept Sam Gunnison's death now. Big Sam was gone, but in a sense he wasn't, because Emmy was here now, and life went on, and even got better, full of promise.

He stepped down and went to Emmy, standing beside her and, putting an arm around her shoulder, holding the future close, while the grass and the trees and the wind and the dust-to-dust welcomed all of them home.

☕ HarperPaperbacks *By Mail*

To complete your Zane Grey collection, check off the titles you're missing and order today!

- ❏ Arizona Ames (0-06-100171-6)................................ $3.99
- ❏ The Arizona Clan (0-06-100457-X)....................... $3.99
- ❏ Betty Zane (0-06-100523-1)................................... $3.99
- ❏ Black Mesa (0-06-100291-7)................................. $3.99
- ❏ Blue Feather and Other Stories (0-06-100581-9)....... $3.99
- ❏ The Border Legion (0-06-100083-3)..................... $3.95
- ❏ Boulder Dam (0-06-100111-2)............................... $3.99
- ❏ The Call of the Canyon (0-06-100342-5).............. $3.99
- ❏ Captives of the Desert (0-06-100292-5)............... $3.99
- ❏ Code of the West (0-06-1001173-2)...................... $3.99
- ❏ The Deer Stalker (0-06-100147-3)........................ $3.99
- ❏ Desert Gold (0-06-100454-5)................................ $3.99
- ❏ The Drift Fence (0-06-100455-3).......................... $3.99
- ❏ The Dude Ranger (0-06-100055-8)....................... $3.99
- ❏ Fighting Caravans (0-06-100456-1)...................... $3.99
- ❏ Forlorn River (0-06-100391-3).............................. $3.99
- ❏ The Fugitive Trail (0-06-100442-1)....................... $3.99
- ❏ The Hash Knife Outfit (0-06-100452-9)............... $3.99
- ❏ The Heritage of the Desert (0-06-100451-0)........ $3.99
- ❏ Knights of the Range (0-06-100436-7)................. $3.99
- ❏ The Last Trail (0-06-100583-5)............................. $3.99
- ❏ The Light of Western Stars (0-06-100339-5)........ $3.99
- ❏ The Lone Star Ranger (0-06-100450-2)................ $3.99
- ❏ The Lost Wagon Train (0-06-100064-7)............... $3.99
- ❏ Majesty's Rancho (0-06-100341-7)....................... $3.99
- ❏ The Maverick Queen (0-06-100392-1).................. $3.99
- ❏ The Mysterious Rider (0-06-100132-5)................. $3.99
- ❏ Raiders of Spanish Peaks (0-06-100393-X)......... $3.99
- ❏ The Ranger and Other Stories (0-06-100587-8)... $3.99
- ❏ The Reef Girl (0-06-100498-7).............................. $3.99
- ❏ Riders of the Purple Sage (0-06-100469-3).......... $3.99